Charles Warren

Faithful Friends

A Sensational Drama

Charles Warren

Faithful Friends
A Sensational Drama

ISBN/EAN: 9783337342821

Printed in Europe, USA, Canada, Australia, Japan

Cover: Foto ©Andreas Hilbeck / pixelio.de

More available books at **www.hansebooks.com**

FAITHFUL FRIENDS,

A

Sensational Drama,

IN

FOUR ACTS.

BY

CHARLES WARREN.

INDEPENDENCE, IOWA.
BULLETIN JOB PRINTING HOUSE.
1890.

CAST OF CHARACTERS.

MISS FLORENCE ESTABROOK, a Southern rose.

MRS. ESTABROOK, mild and gentle.

AUNT DINAH.

MOTHER CAREY, one who has suffered.

LITTLE MANDA.

A. LITTLE SHORT, amateur detective and auctioneer.

HIRAM ESTABROOK, one of the old stock.

UNCLE JEFF, faithful and true.

DADDY CAREY, a bird of prey.

RASTUS, just doing nothing.

ROYCE GARDNER, a man of schemes.

FRANK WOODRUFF, his pal.

　　　　Negroes, Guests, Speculators, Moonshiners &c.

FAITHFUL FRIENDS.

ACT I.

SCENE 1.—*Exterior of southern plantation homestead. Set house with steps going up* L. *Gate. Picket fence running across stage in 4. Garden set of furniture. Set trees if practicable.*

CHORUS FOR RISE OF CURTAIN.

Dere will be no mournful parting,
    Dere be no sisters sighing,
When we once get on the golden shore.
    All will be gladly singing,
Music will be merry ringing,
    When we once get on de golden shore;
No money care and sorrow,
    And no grief we'll ever borrow,
When once we get on de golden shore.

Den wait with patience in your heart,
      Wait, Wait,
And never let your courage depart,
      Wait, Wait,
For ebery colored sinner,
    Will have preserve for his dinner,
When we once get on de golden shore.

Enter HIRAM ESTABROOK *from house — stands on steps.*

ESTA. Here, what is all this noise about? Rastus! Rastus! Just like that lazy, stupid nigger—never about when he's wanted and always in the way when he's not. Rastus, I say! Well, when I catch him I'll have his black hide tanned until he cries for mercy. Ah! here is what I was in search of; the New Orleans paper. (*Takes the paper and sits down.*) To-day I have a task before me that I dislike exceedingly, but it must be done. I must be firm, determined; my brief experience on the cotton market, at New Orleans, has cut a pretty hole in my bank account, and to make good my losses I must dispose of some of the younger niggers. They're lying around here in droves and they would never be missed. (*Noise outside.*) What's that? (*Rises, goes and looks off* R.) Why, it's that rascally Rastus—as usual turnsng up when he's not wanted.

RASTUS. (*Outside.*) Go on yo' fool niggers—nigger, nigger yo'se'f. Don't you go pesterin' 'round me yo' h'ar, or dar is gwine be a black funeral and sum ob you niggers won't hear de singin'; sum ob yo' ride in de fust kart. (*Backs into Estabrook.*) Golly, if 'tain't massa —'scuse me massa, I dun didn't notice you in my pertubation.

ESTA.   So you've come at last.   What have you been doing? "Jess doin' nuffin," doing nothing, have you, you lazy nigger?

RASTUS.   'Scuse me massa, I ain't dun gwine be lazy—but I'se not bery foolish to work.

ESTA.   Do you know what I think of doing with you, you scoundrel?

RASTUS.   Ain't got de least wise recomembrance, massa.

ESTA.   I think I'll give you a good whipping.

RASTUS.   'Tain't no use, massa, you'se dun whoop me more'n fifty times and I'se more fool dan eber.

ESTA.   Well, then I'll sell you.

RASTUS.   Please doan sell me, massa; nobody gwine buy me— fool nigger doan know nuffin.   Dem smart niggers dey got sold, dey hab to work too, cause dey got sense —I'se foolish—doan keer, I'se glad on it.

ESTA.   None of your impudence now; get about your work.

RASTUS.   Yes sah; I'se bery busy jess now, I'se 'bassador.

ESTA.   A what?   Explain yourself, you scoundrel.

RASTUS.   A 'bassador, sah—a fellow what comes to a fellow from 'nudder fellow who doan know de fellow what he' comin' to from 'nudder fellow.   Dat's what business I'se in.

ESTA.   What do you mean by this nonsense?

RASTUS.   Couldn't done 'splain mo' massa.   Uncle Jeff he done wants to speak to you 'ticklar and he asked me to ask you ef he mout speak to you.

ESTA.   Uncle Jeff; what can he want?   Some complaint -these niggers never know when they're well off.

RASTUS.   Dem niggers what's got sense dun gwine grumblin' more'n all de foolish niggers in de worl'.

ESTA.   I suppose I must see him; where is he?

RASTUS.   He's waitin' jest at de door, massa.

ESTA.   Tell him to come here-- be brief.

RASTUS.   I'se gwine tell him massa.   Ain't I de foolish nigger.
                                                      (*Exit* R. 2 E.

ESTA.   Now what can this man want with me?   If it isn't one annoyance it's another, and yet people cite the southern planter as the happiest man in the world.

RASTUS *enters* R. 2 E., *followed by* UNCLE JEFF.

RASTUS.   (*Aside to* JEFF.)   Dar is massa.   Don't be skeered; he make a mighty fuss and scold heap but he's good to nigger.   Jess go and sed sumfin to him.   (*Goes up stage.*)

JEFF. (*Coming down and bowing to* ESTABROOK, *hat in hand.*) If yo' please, mossa.

ESTA. Well, what is it, Jeff? Come, be quick about it, I've no time to waste.

JEFF. If yo' please sah, me and my ol' woman down at de cabin, heer'd you was gwine to sell some of de hands, and de oberseer done sed dat our little Manda was gwine to be sold and gwine down de riber.

ESTA. Yes, Jeff, that's true Is that all?

JEFF. All, mossa, yes sah, dat's all. All my ol' woman's pleasure in life. Dat chile is all de one we got, and I done come to ask yo' mossa, please not take her away from us. She's only six years old, mossa, she can't do much and won't bring a heap, but if yo' send her away it'll mighty nigh break ol' woman's heart and mine.

ESTA. You must not bother me with such talk. The niggers must be sold and she among them. She's young and in a few weeks you'll not miss her.

JEFF. Not miss her, mossa; den mossa, we'd never miss de sun if it was to be forever behind de clouds; we'd never miss de singin' of dem birds in de magnolia, nor de flowers in de woods and fields.

ESTA. Enough of such sentiment. It's useless — the child must go. My losses have been severe of late and I cannot afford to have this crowd of young niggers about, eating me out of house and home.

JEFF. But, oh, please mossa, spare our Manda to us. Think if some one took good Missy Florence from you!

ESTA. You black scoundrel, how dare you compare your child to mine — your little black brat to the heiress of this estate.

JEFF. 'Scuse me mossa for sayin' sumfin wrong, but we lubs our Manda de same as yo' lub good Missy Florence. Our skins are black but we got feelins, mossa; our hearts may not be black, mossa.

ESTA. You have said too much. Go back to your cabin; the child must be sold and this very day. If I had had a desire to let her stay, you have spoiled your chance by your sentimental whining. Be off I say.

JEFF. But mossa, jus' think —

ESTA. No, I say, and if I hear you grumbling and whining among the other niggers, you'll not only lose your brat, but you'll get fifty lashes besides on your bare hide. Now go; I will hear no more whining from you.

JEFF. Yes, mossa. 'Scuse me for beggin' for my chile. (*turning aside.*) May de good Lord in Heaben neber cause him sich misery as dis is to me.   (*Exit*, R. 2 E.

ESTA. That nigger wants a good whipping. The idea of his

daring to compare his love for his brat with mine for Florence, my heart's idol—my only child and daughter. It's nearly time for her to be at home. Rastus! Where is that damned nigger? Rastus!

RASTUS. (*Comes from house eating a piece of pie.*) Golly, dis good pie, bes' I'be had dis whole year. Did yo' call me Massa Estabrook?

ESTA. Did I call? Yes, I yelled. Don't you know enough to be within call? Where were you and what were you doing out to the barn?

RASTUS. Jus' doin' nuffin'.

ESTA. Just doing nothing as usual, eh?

RASTUS. (*Aside.*) I don't know nuffin'—I'se foolish.

ESTA. What time did Miss Florence go for her ride?

RASTUS. 'Bout an hour ago, massa, and golly, how she did go down de lane on dat new horse you bought her— and ef you'd see'd de way dat ar dog Frank keep right at dat horse's heels, and neber min' nobody callin' him, you'd a dest laff'd. I'se done laff'd myse'f all day. (*Aside.*) I ain't got no sense, I'se foolish.

ESTA. When she returns tell her I expect a number of people here to-day, as I am going to auction off some of the negroes. Tell her to see that everything necessary for their entertainment is ready. I am going down to the quarters to look over the surplus you understand?   (*Exit, L. 2 E.*)

RASTUS. Yes sah, massa, cose I un'stand. (*Aside.*) He tinks caze I'se no sense, I kaint hear. Golly, but massa is rlled dis morning. He's gwine have sumbody here 'n when dey come den is de time dis'yer chile sneaks inter de house 'n fills hisse'f full of cakes and pies and all sich trimmins. Golly, den I'll sleep and sleep, and when massa calls I'se gwine say, "Rastus doan heah yo' He's done takin' good slumber. Fast asleep I is." (*Lies down stage centre, snoring.*)

SHORT. (*heard outside.*) Ah, this is the way. All right sir— much obliged—see you again. (*rushes in* R. 3 E: *stumbles over* RASTUS, *who rises to hands and knees.*) Ah, what's this; a brilliant specimen of the overworked negro of fiction. Arise Senegambian, I would fain communicate with thee. Ah, I see what you are going to ask, who am I? "Who is you?" Exactly, I'll tell you my name. A. Short, a northern gentleman cruizing in Southern society; auctioneer by profession, but with a soul that yearns for greater things. Ah yes, it yearns, it yearns, it yearns.

RASTUS. Look heah, massa man, ef you's gwine to hab de colic cramps, yo' bettah go right straight in de house to ol' missus 'n git sumfin.

SHORT. You mistake emotion for cramps; very natural.

RASTUS. Don't know nuffin 'bout no 'motion. I ain't got no sense, I'se foolish.

SHORT. Sable philosopher, let me grasp your digit. I have seen hundreds of men in your exact mental condition, but you are the first to come out like a man and acknowledge the corn. But tell me, is this the house of Mr. Hiram Estabrook?

RASTUS. You done guess dat de fust time. Dis am de place ob Mistah Hi'um Estabrook, jess sho as yer bo'n, dat's what it is.

SHORT. And you, I take it, are one of his niggers?

RASTUS. No sah, nobody nigger bu: de debil. I'se black stained gemman, I is, dat's me.

SHORT. Where is your master?

RASTUS. He's done gone down to de quarters. He's 'spectin' sumbody and he tole me fo' to tell Miss Florence—well, I 'clar to goodness ef I ain't fo'got dat what massa tole me for to tell Miss Florence — what was dat.?

SHORT. Florence—who is she, his sister?

RASTUS. Go on, mistah. Sistah nuffin—she's his only da'teh, and massa and missus tink dar is but one person on de top ob dis'yer ground, and dat's Miss Florence. She mighty gay; yo' h'ar me, she is.

SHORT. This grows interesting; what is she like, Sambo?

RASTUS. Doan go make maulk my name. I ain't no Samo—I'se Rastus, I is, what's foolish.

SHORT. All right Sambo, I'll call you Rastus. What is this young lady like?

RASTUS. I couldn't tol' you sah. She's like honey and possum, sweet 'taters and fire-crackers all togeder I 'spec—I'se talkin'; yo' h'ar me?

SHORT. And where is she now?

RASTUS. She's habin' her mo'nin' ride. De sun neber git bery high 'fo dat lady is on her hoss and her cog at de hoss's heels, flyin' fom one place t'oder like de win'--no ruff wind, kase she allers good.

SHORT. Well, I will see this prodigy. Tell Mr. Estabrook that the gentleman whom he sent for to sell off his extra slaves awaits him. Fly Sambo.

RASTUS. All right sah, Rastus is flyin' Don't know no Sambo; Sambo soun'sifies like lazy, but Rastus—Rastus is jess breakin' his back a flyin'. (*Exit very slowly into house during this speech.*)

SHORT. (*looking after him.*) Rastus, your wings are not mates; he is slow, just like the country. It's in the air. This job promises to be interesting. Old man in difficulties, probably, as he wants to sell off some of his slaves—pretty daughter; spoiled child without a doubt, with lovers by the score. This ought to be just in my way.

Now if there is only some mystery to clear up, some diabolical plot to thwart— (*enter* RASTUS *from steps, just to hear the last words.*) oh how I would revel in a murder!

RASTUS.   Oh Lord! dat man bad; I'se gwine lebe.   (*Exit* L. 2 E., *very much frightened.*)

SHORT.   (*turning about quickly.*)   Why, what's the matter? (*looks toward steps and sees* MRS. ESTABROOK, *who has entered—aside.*) Ah, the fair creature's mother, no doubt.

MRS. ESTA.   You will pardon my servant sir; he is a little eccentric at times.

SHORT.   Oh yes, he confided his troubles to me a moment since. (*touching his head significantly.*)   Foolish, perhaps.   This is——?

MRS. ESTA.   Mrs. Estabrook.

SHORT.   Allow me to introduce myself—A. Short, auctioneer, here at the request of your husband, professionally.

MRS. ESTA.   An auctioneer here!   Why, I have heard nothing of an auction here.

SHORT.   Do not speak of an auctioneer in such an appalling manner.   It is my profession through poverty, not inclination.   Did I follow the beat of my own desires, I'd seek the counterfeiter in his lair, and I would wade in lashings of gurgling gore.

MRS. ESTA.   I don t understand you.

SHORT   You do not grasp my meaning; to bidders I would say, bid me good-bye and go, and I would devote my life to the glorious cause of justice.   I would have a secret star in my inside pocket. and I'd detect everything from a brutal murder to a piece of cheese.   You don't happen to have a mystery you want unravelled, a mysterious murder you want looked up?

MTS. ESTA.   Sir!

SHORT.   Just my luck; I'll have to stick to my old business, auctioneering; going, going, gone,

MRS. ESTA   I am sorry we cannot oblige you in your desires, Mr. Short, but here comes Mr. Estabrook with one of our neighbors; he can doubtless give you information regarding your business here. So, for the present, I wish you a good morning.   (*Exit into house.*

SHORT.   Good morning. (*lifts hat politely.*)   Cool and bracing but here comes my man; now to ascertain what he wishes me to knock down, professionally speaking.   He seems in animated conversation with his companion.   What if they should be talking of a hidden crime.   I'll do it!   Secreted behind this tree I will listen to their words, and it may prove a daring robbery at the very least.

(*Hides behind tree.*

Enter ESTABROOK *and* GARDNER.

ESTA. (*as he enters.* It is useless to press your suit farther with me, Mr. Gardner. Mrs. Estabrook and myself are, as you are aware, bound up in our only daughter, and when she leaves us it must be to marry some one whom she truly loves and who will make her a good husband.

GARDNER. But Mr. Estabrook, I hardly think I am distasteful to Miss Florence. I deemed it my duty, however, to speak first to you.

ESTA. I appreciate that; but I have fully determined not to lead her choice in any way. If she loves you and her mother and myself are satisfied, she will be yours. I can only say. go win if you can.

GARDNER. Thanks for that assurance, Mr. Estabrook. You will pardon me, but I have learned from reliable sources that you have become temporarily embarrassed. Now you know my income is ample, and should you use your influence with Miss Florence, any request of yours would be granted.

ESTA. Excuse me Mr. Gardner, you have been misinformed. Hiram Estabrook makes no obligations that he cannot meet, and in any case my daughter's hand is not for sale. Good morning.
(*Exit into house.*

SHORT. (*head appearing from behind tree.*) Cool and bracing— this is very interesting.

GARDNER. (*looking after* ESTABROOK.) That's like these shabby genteel gentlemen, poor and proud. But pride goeth before a fall, and that girl will yet be my wife. She is just the sort of girl I like— courageous as a lion, spiteful as a wolf and as cunning as a wild cat. Just the sort of woman a man of my disposition likes to tame, and bend to do his bidding. My bluff to assist him does not go. It was a bold one for me, for had he accepted I should have been at a loss to know how to have helped him. I am up to my ears in debt, and my creditors are already making my life miserable. This difficulty of Estabrook's is only temporary; could I but win his daughter's hand, her marriage portion would save me from ruin, and at the old man's death I would come into this estate. Whatever obstacle arises in my path, she must and shall be mine.
(*Exit* R. I E.

SHORT. (*coming from behind tree.*) I know it is contrary to the rules of etiquette to be an eaves-dropper, but this certainly looks interesting. Poor father, charming daughter, and suitor not any too strong with the aged parent. Oh, I may strike a case here after all; but there's no mystery, it's open as the day, nothing to detect—just my luck. Cool and bracing.

ESTA. (*heard within.*) You say he is in the garden. I will find him. (*Enters from house.*)

SHORT. (*approaching him.*) Mr. Estabrook, I believe?

ESTA. Yes; and you — Mr. Short?

SHORT   A. Little Short, a Northern cruiser in Southern waters; auctioneer at present, but with aspirations.   Ah, I need say no more, I was informed by Mr. Glenny of Glencoe that you desired my professional services this morning, so I rode over.

ESTA.   Yes, Mr. Short; I am glad to see you.   You have been highly recommended.

SHORT.   Pleased sir; highly delighted.   Now what am I to have the pleasure of knocking down, or rather selling, this morning?

ESTA.   I wish to sell a number of my young negroes.   I dislike the task more than I can say, as there has not been a slave sold on this plantation for years.   Now, however it becomes necessary.

SHORT.   I understand, sir.   Bad crops, heavy expenses, profits on wrong side of the ledger &c. &c. &c.

ESTA.   No, you are mistaken.   I cannot blame nature; she has been more than kind.   Crops have been good and the plantation has been more than ordinarily successful; I have only to blame myself. I was led into a speculation and risked more than I could safely do, without endangering the estate.   The affair was unfortunate and I lost heavily.   As security I gave my note for three thousand dollars. This note has fallen into the hands of the brokers and it must be promptly met or action will be commenced against me at once.   I have delayed in the matter for some time, but now I find that my only resource is the young negroes.   Therefore they must be sold and at once.

SHORT.   Excuse me Mr. Estabrook; our short acquaintance hardly warrants my presumption, but I have dabbled in law a bit myself, and might be of service to you.   Have you a memorandum of the note with you?

ESTA. (*takes out pocket-book*.)   Yes, here; I took it from my safe this morning, but did not examine it closely.

SHORT. (*takes memorandum.*)   Ah, yes, $3,000.   Why, my dear sir, this note must be met within three days, and payment must be made at New Orleans.   You have delayed in this matter until it is nearly too late.

ESTA.   It must be met, otherwise it would be my lasting disgrace, and I could never hold up my head again.

SHORT.   Then you must act speedily.   We are two days from New Orleans by boat, and the last mail packet leaves Roscoe at nine to-night.   You must take action at once.

ESTA.   I will; but hush, not a word to my wife; here she comes.

Enter MRS. ESTABROOK *from house.*

My dear, I have just been talking business with Mr. Short, and have prevailed upon him to remain and dine with us.

MRS ESTA. I am glad to hear it. Ah, our neighbor, Mr. Gardner is returning I see.

Enter GARDNER. L. 1 E.

GARDNER. I am pleased to greet you, gentlemen

ESTA. Mr. Gardner, Mr. Short. This gentleman has driven over from Glencoe to manage my sale to-day. I trust you will remain.

GARDNER. (*to Short.* Pleased to know you, sir. Been in this country long?

SHORT. No; just cruising about in search of bids.

GARDNER. From the north, eh?

SHORT. Yes, from the land of blizzards and snow storms, and keenly alive to the beauties of the south.

ESTA. (*going up stage.*) Where's that boy Rastus?

MRS. ESTA. He was here a moment ago. I reckon he has gone to look for Florence. He is almost as watchful of her as her dog Frank is.

SHORT. Your daughter is fond of outdoor life it seems, Mr. Estabrook?

ESTA. Yes, she lives in the open air, swims like a duck, shoots like a Nimrod and is the best horsewoman for twenty miles around. (*shouts and cheers outside.*) What's that? Ah! if you don't believe it look at her on her homeward ride. Sits in the saddle like a cavalryman. She's perfect mistress of the rein.

MUSIC.— *Shouts as* FLORENCE *enters followed by* RASTUS *and negroes.* GARDNER *rushes to help her dismount, but she jumps down before he gets to her side.*

FLOR. No, thanks, Mr. Gardner, I have been taught to help myself. (*stands up stage centre patting horse's head.*) Oh, papa. I've had such a ride, up hill and down dale, scurrying through the brush and Tony leaping over fences. I can never thank you enough for this good; kind horse. He is all spirit and fire, yet under rein as docile as a lamb, What a temper he had! He tried to show it, but when he found that mine was equal to his he gracefully yielded, and now we are the best of friends. Arn't we dear old fellow? (*caresses horse.—dog comes up to her.*) And I must not forget my other friend, faithful Frank. (*pats the dog.*) What a time we have had. Frank running like mad in his attempt to race with Tony. Oh, you beauty, come and kiss me. I do think a deal of him; I know he does of me as well. He and Tony are great friends; we are all friends, faithful friends.

SHORT. (*aside.*) Oh, that dog don't know his luck.

ESTA. Florence, my child, your enthusiasm has caused you to forget our guests. Mr. Short, my daughter, Miss Florence.

SHORT.   Charmed, delighted, Miss Estabrook to greet one of nature's beauties.   It is a delightful experience to meet a natural woman, after the affectations of modern society.

FLOR.   You are very kind.   Of society I know very little. There are few young folks about here, and my society, aside from my dear papa and mamma, is my horse and dog.

GARDNER.   You enjoy your rides, Miss Florence?

FLOR.   Indeed I do.   What can be grander than the cool, bracing air of a spring morning, and a ride on the back of a noble horse, over a road fragrant with budding magnolias; the air sweet with the song of birds, and the company of a noble animal who seems to know your very thoughts, and changes his pace in accordance with them. (*Frank, the dog goes toward* GARDNER, *who strikes him a light blow with his cane. Frank growls and barks.*) Don't strike him, Mr. Gardner, please.   No one ever whips my dog.

GARDNER.   Dogs and niggers must be whipped to make them obey.

FLOR.   Then your experience, I am compelled to say, must have been with curs.

SHORT. *(aside.)*   Cool and bracing, again.

ESTA.   Gardner is right about niggers.   They are always annoying, lazy, good for nothing and object to being sold.   Jeff, this morning, annoyed me because I am going to sell his child, Manda.

GARDNER.   You allow too many privileges, Mr. Estabrook. Those black rascals have no feeling; it s animal cunning.   They want sympathy –those negro mothers care more for a pipe of tobacco than they do for a child.   Once out of sight, out of mind with them.

SHORT. *(to* FLORENCE.)   Your dog—Frank you call him—seems to be very intelligent, and, I dare say, thinks a great deal of you.

FLOR.   Intelligent!   He can do anything but talk, and he loves me devotedly.   Indeed yes, I believe all that a poor animal is capable of.   Just see what I have taught him to do.   (*ties horse to post in* C., *comes down stage and sits on rustic bench or chair.*)   Frank, bring me my horse. (*dog goes and unties horse and leads him to his mistress.*) Good dog (*caressing him.*)   Now lead him to RASTUS. (*Frank obeys.*) Come here. Frank; Aunt Dinah, bring me my jacket from the hall. (AUNT DINAH *brings jacket from house.*) Now I will show you what an expert pickpocket Frank is; but don't be alarmed.   He will not take anything unless he is bidden, or that does not belong to him. (*hangs up jacket and places envelope in pocket.*)   Now, Frank get me my letter. (*dog goes to jacket and brings the envelope.*)   See, isn't he a good one. (*caressing dog.*)   It surely pays to spend a little time educating a noble animal.

ESTA.   That is enough now.   Florence, Mrs. Estabrook, will you see that lunch is prepared at once. Come, gentlemen, I will show you the negroes in question, and after lunch the sale will begin at once. I think we may as well have it here.

FLOR. (*to* MRS. ESTA.) Sale! What does he mean, mamma?

MRS. ESTA. (*aside.*) Hush child, it is some business transaction of your father's.

ESTA. This way, gentlemen. (*leads the way up stage, followed by* SHORT. GARDNER *lingers behind.*)

MRS. ESTA. (*going toward house.*) Come, Florence, you must change your dress and decoraate the table for luncheon,

(*Exit into house.*

FLOR. What sale? I have never heard of this before. A sale. What can it mean?

GARDNER. (*coming down to her.*) I will tell you, Miss Florence.

FLOR. Mr. Gardner, you here?

GARDNER. Yes; I left your father and his friends on a trivial pretext, that I might return and have a few moments conversation with you.

FLOR. What can you have to say to me?

GARDNER. Something that concerns the happiness of my future life. Miss Florence, as you know, I am a bachelor tolerably well circumstanced. Life to me is very lonely withal; I never had a thought of marriage until your fresh young beauty impressed me. Then all powerful love crept into my life and I knew that I could never be happy unless you became my wife.

FLOR Mr. Gardner, you astonish me. I really do not understand such language.

GARDNER. I have proceeded in the regular way. I asked your father's permission this morning, and he said his consent depended entirely upon your answer. Now tell me, Miss Florence, will you fill my heart with the greatest joy man can experience, and promise to become my wife.

FLOR. I am sorry, Mr. Gardner, but I cannot.

GARDNER. Think it over —don't hurry. Give me your answer later.

FLOR. No delay is necessary. I must give you my final refusal now.

GARDNER. But give me some reason. Are your affections elsewhere engaged? Do you dislike me?

FLOR. You ask me and I will answer candidly. I do not like you. Any man who speaks slightingly of a parent's love for his child or abuses a dear, good faithful dog, can never be numbered among my friends.

GARDNER. Am I to understand that because I spoke of the whip for niggers and dogs, and slightly struck your dog, I am therefore to lose your friendship?

FLOR. You will not lose it, because you never had it. I tell you plainly, Mr. Gardner, I do not like you, I never did and I never will. Good morning. (*goes toward house.*)

FLOR. One moment, Miss Florence; it is evident you do not know what love is.

FLOR. Oh, yes I do, I have read its definition in books;

"What is love, if thou wouldst be taught,
Thy heart should teach alone;
Two souls with but a single thought,
Two hearts that beat as one."

GARDNER. Do not mock me. You have refused my love—have you ever heard of tender love suddenly changing to deadly hatred. You renounce me as a friend; beware of me as an enemy. Your father is in difficulties; his honor is at stake and should his obligations not be met, the haughty, reserved Hiram Estabrook will be the object at which the finger of scorn will be pointed, I was ready to assist him, but your rejection of my proposal convinces me that my sympathy is entirely misplaced.

FLOR. It is misplaced, Mr. Gardner. Whatever trouble my father is in, I am sure he would accept no assistance from you. He would sooner bend his pride to the dust—would sooner beg from door to door than have his daughter marry such a man as I think you are.

GARDNER. You are excited, Miss Estabrook. I will leave you and rejoin your father. Remember what you have decided. We are enemies. It is to be war to the knife. Good morning.

(*Exit through gate, raising his hat.*

FLOR. Oh! how I would like to scratch out his eyes. Ah! if I was only a man, I would pitch into him and take as much comfort in hitting him as he did in striking my poor dog. But what does it all mean- papa in trouble, a sale to take place; what can be the matter?

Enter AUNT DINAH from house.

AUNT DINAH. Oh Missy Flo'nce, don't let dem take her from me, sabe my little chile. Missy do—oh, ol' Dinah's heart 'll done break. (*falls on knees, beseechingly.*)

FLOR. (*taking her hand.*) Why, Aunt Dinah, what's the matter? Tell me.

AUNT DINAH. Matter, missy; ain't you done heerd dat all de chillen as kaint work gwine to be sol' to-day and sent down de riber, and 'mong dem dey's gwine sell my little gal, Mundy. My little baby, dat I neber tought mossa would sell from me. Lose dat baby, oh, Dinah sho'ly die.

FLOR. Going to sell your Manda? Impossible! Why, Uncle Jeff and you have been my father's most faithful servants and I am sure that he will never do such a cruel thing as to take your baby from you.

AUNT DINAH. Speak to him, missy. Pray to him to spar' my my little chile, and I will bress yo' to de longest day ob dis poo' ol' Dinah's life.

FLOR. I will, aunt Dinah. Now go back to the kitchen and I will see my father, and persuade and do all I can with him not to sell Manda. Dry your eyes and keep up a good heart; all will be well, we must hope.

AUNT DINAH. T'ank you missy. Lo'd bress yo' pretty face and keep yo' from all harm. De Lo'd bress yo'—Dinah always know yo' got a kind heart. (*Exit into house.*

FLOR. Poor old woman. It would indeed a blow to them to part with the little one whom they have made their hearts' idol No, they must not take the little child; they shall not sell her. For that I'll be bound, if it is in my power to save her.

MRS. ESTA. (*from within.*) Florence! Florence!

FLOR. There's mother calling. I forgot what she told me· Yes, mamma, I am coming.

Enter MRS. ESTABROOK *on steps.*

MRS. ESTA. Florence, child, why do you not come to decorate the table? The gentlemen are coming and you are still in your riding habit.

FLOR. Excuse me this time, that's a dear good mother. I have been very much occupied here—but here are papa's friends. I will tell you about it at another time.

Enter ESTABROOK, SHORT *and* GARDNER.

SHORT. (*as he enters.*) And a very comfortable place you have, Mr. Estabrook. It is little wonder that you are envied by half the country around. A productive plantation. everything in good repair and really a surplus of negroes. You are indeed to be envied.

ESTA. Providence has indeed been kind to me, Mr, Short, yet life on a prosperous plantation is not all serenity, I suppose.

GARDNNR. No, we can never tell. Outside appearances are of_ ten deceptive. Like a woman's pretty face, they are sometimes the mask for an ungrateful heart.

SHORT. Ah, I must differ with you, Mr. Gardner. There must be no slurring allusions to the sex that all should love, honor and cherish, especially when we have two such charming representatives present.

FLOR. Mr. Gardner is evidently a cynic regarding we poor women. Cynicism and disppointment generally go together.

MRS. ESTA   Florence, don't be rude.   Mr. Estabrook, the luncheon is served, and if you will show the gentlemen in—

ESTA.   Certainly, my dear.   Mr. Gardner, Mr. Short, just follow my wife.   We will have a drop of brandy, a bit of something to eat and will then proceed with the sale.

MRS. ESTA *(as she enters the house.)*   This way, gentlemen.

SHORT.   With pleasure, Mrs. Estabrook.   *(Exit into house.*

GARDNER. *(as he reaches door.)*   I hope we will have the pleasure of your society, Miss Florence.

FLOR.   In just a moment—I have a word to say to father.

GARDNER.   We will await you with impatience. *(Exit in house*

ESTA.   You wish to speak with me, Florence.

FLOR.   Yes, papa, I wish to ask of you above all, one favor.

ESTA.   Will not another time do, as well, my daughter— go in and get dressed.   I suppose some new trinket has caught your eye. Well, we'll see about it; but now I must entertain our guests.   You know there is nothing in reason that I would refuse my daughter.

FLOR.   Do you really mean that, papa.

ESTA.   Certainly, my child.

FLOR,   Then don't sell Aunt Dinah's little Manda.

ESTA.   What!   Have those old fools been to you with their troubles?   I must put a stop to their complainings at once, or the whole plantation will be in a state of discontent and trouble.

FLOR.   No, papa, don't do anything cruel. It was only Aunt Dinah, who has served you so faithfully and well all her life, and was my black "mammy;" who came to me and tearfully pleaded that I would ask you to spare her Manda.   Please do, papa, for my sake.

ESTA.   Florence, you do not know what you are talking about. You must not interfere with my business affairs.   Anything in reason you ask me will be granted, but I say no to this and ask you to say nothing more about it.

FLOR.   But papa, think of the unhappiness, the misery you will cause by this determination; you separate a child from its parents, you break a poor old mother's heart and darken her declining years for a few paltry dollars.   Please save her child, papa--oh, poor Aunt Dinah!   Think, papa, of the grief you cause her.   Yes, a living death; to see that poor old woman unhaappy will ever make me so.

ESTA.   Florence, you do not understand the circumstances., and I cannot explain now.   You must be satisfied with the knowledge that I think it best, and that no pleading on your part will change my mind I must have money.

FLOR.   If you need money, sell my horse, Tony, that you gave

me, and which I so highly prize. Rather than have that child sold
and sent down the river, I would gladly part with him. Take the
precious jewels that you have given me; everything I have will go
freely, now that my sympathy is enlisted for my old black mammy
and her little child.

ESTA. Don't be foolish, child. Don't let your sympathy rob
you of reason. Thousands of niggers are being sold every year —
what is one more or less to you or me?

FLOR. Papa, I don't wish to give you cause to be angry with
me for persisting in this appeal, but I feel that if you sell the little
one some great trouble will come over our home. The prayers of
the lowly are heard above, and should you inflict this great wrong
upon your faithful and inoffensive servants you may perhaps suffer
in some similar way. Some of your loved ones may be taken from
you, and you made to feel the torture of a more painful separation.

ESTA. Enough of this nonsense. You know that when I have
made up my mind, I will not change it. Keep your sympathy; I
dare say it is not appreciated, but let me hear no more of this I've
a great mind to have the overseer give that old woman fifty lashes
for going to you and playing upon your feelings — but we must go to
our guests—come.

FLOR. No, papa, I hardly feel equal to the task of entertaining
them. I will have Rastus bring around Tony and I will have a ride
down the road; perhaps it will make me feel better.

ESTA. As you like; but remember, no more nonsense about
that brat.   (*Exit into house.*

FLOR. He is inflexible. I never knew my father could be so
cruel. I can never bear to see the little one sold. The sight of the
weeping mother, and the heartbroken father would make me miséra-
ble. I must go somewhere, anywhere, until this wretched sale is
over, and then try to forget it.

Enter RASTUS, *cautiously.*

RASTUS. Missy, Missy; hush!

FLOR. What is it, Rastus?

RASTUS. Is he gone?

FLOR. Gone—who?

RASTUS. Dat feller wot wus a lookin' fer blood; he's got mighty ebil eye, he's bad man, missy, sho' he s. He done want to wade
in goah. I'se foolish, I is, but if dat'ar man rub up agin me, Ras'
gwine break fo de qua'ters sho'.

FLOR. Why, Rastus, you're crazy.

RASTUS. No, missy I'se des foolish; but is he done gone?

FLOR. Of whom are you speaking?

RASTUS. Dat sho't man. He calls hisse'f Mistah Sho't, all de time sayin', goin', goin', gone; I done hope his stayin' 'round hyer 'll be as sho't as his name.

FLOR. Oh, you mean Mr. Short. Why, he is not a bad man; you can see that by his face

RASTUS. Dat's all right, missy, but dere's sumfin' 'bout dem ebil eyes ob his'n dat make me na vous, sho' 'nuff.

FLOR. Why, he is an auctioneer.

RASTUS. Da's what's de mattah wid 'im. He's done knockin' down so much 'round yer dat he wont be sa'sfied, 'n bim'by h'es gwine murder somebody.

FLOR. Don't be frightened, he won't harm you.

RASTUS. 'Deed he won't missy; he's got'r ketch me fust. I ain't 'fraid, 'deed I ain't; ef he git sassy ter me, I'll—jus' lef him alone an' lebe myse'f, sho'.

SHORT. (*heard within.*) Very good; excellent, but I will step into the garden.

RASTUS. Yer he done comes now. 'Scuse me, missy, I'se got 'po'tant business to 'tend to out yer.   (*Exit hastily.*

FLOR. Poor Rastus, how frightened he is. But I must slip down to the stables and get Tony. But let me think. Will I let them sell that little child? No! I'll try my best to save her for Aunt Dinah's sake, but how—let me think. I wonder if papa would be angry if—never mind I'll do it, and whatever may be the consequences, I will save the child for those old servants, if possible.
                                                    (*Exit*, R. 1 E.

Enter RASTUS.—*Music heard in house.*

RASTUS. (*stepping awkwardly about.*) Oh, how I des lub to waltz. (*music stops.*) Say, play waltz some mo' (*music starts up lively* RASTUS *commences to waltz, ends with a breakdown, during which*
          Enter ESTABROOK, GARDNER *and* SHORT.
(RASTUS *not seeing them, collides with* ESTABROOK.) Golly! ef 'taint massa!   (*Exit hurriedly.*

SHORT. (*laughing.*) Capital, Mr. Estabrook, the best I ever heard. After a satisfying lunch and a good bottle of wine, one feels on very good terms with the world—but now to business. Where shall we have the sale?

ESTA. I think here. I see a number of our neighbors are now at the quarters, and several speculators from Glencoe have been looking over the negroes. Rastus! Rastus!
                    Enter RASTUS.

RASTUS. Wus yo' callin' me massa?

ESTA. Yes, you black scoundrel; come here. What have been doing?

RASTUS. Jus' doin' nuffin'.

ESTA. Doing nothing, were you? I caught you here dancing a few moments ago.

RASTUS. Jus' jumpin' 'round to cure de stumick ache

ESTA. Come here or I'll make you jump with the back ache. Come here, quick, I say.

RASTUS. (aside.) Dar is Mistah Sho't man. I'se done skeered ob him.

ESTA. What a stupid brute—now it's settled. I'll sell you and down the river you go.

RASTUS. Oh, please massa, don't sell Rastus.

ESTA. Tell Brown, the overseer, that the sale will be held here. Have them bring up the niggers and invite the gentlemen to step this way.

RASTUS. 'Deed I will, massa. (aside.) Dey won't sell dis nigga; ain't got no sense. I'se bery foolish. (Exit L. U. E.

GARDNER. (to ESTABROOK.) We missed Miss Florence at luncheon, Mr. Estabrook. Was the fatigue of her ride this morning too much for her?

ESTA. No, but she has a foolish idea in her head regarding one of the slaves I am to sell.

GARDNER. What is that? She seems to be very sensible for a girl of her age.

ESTA. She usually is, but her sympathies have been worked upon by an old black couple who do not wish to part with their child. She has asked me not to sell it, but it is too late now. The list has been made out and must be adhered to.

GARDNER You are quite right. This mawkish sentiment about nigger's hearts and feelings is nonsense. But here are the niggers.

Enter Supers, Children, Negroes to be sold, Plantation hands, Overseers, Speculators &c.

SHORT. (standing well down L. C.) Gentlemen: I am here today at the request of your worthy neighbor, Mr. Estabrook, to call your attention to a lot of young negroes. the finest for their age in this market. It is unusual, as you know, for Mr. Estabrook to part with his people. and as a result he has the best trained and hardest working negroes for miles around. The number has so increased, however, that some must be disposed of. So here is your golden opportunity to purchase the very best negroes in the couutry The first lot I will offer consists of a boy and girl, age 10 and 8, sound in wind and limb, will soon make excellent good workers. Now what am I offered for the two—what am I offered?

VOICE. One hundred dollars.

SHORT. One hundred—do I hear two? One hundred, one hundred—

VOICE. One fifty.

SHORT. Thank you for small favors, sir; but won't some one say two hundred?

VOICE. Two hundred.

SHORT. Thank you; there's a man of good judgment; can see a good thing when it stands before him. Gentlemen, this is the chance of your lives. Who says three hundred; won't some one say three hundred; worth five hundred if a dollar. Open your eyes and see for yourselves.

VOICE. Two fifty.

SHORT. Good again—two fifty once, two fifty twice—

VOICE. Three hundred.

SHORT. Ah, there is still hope. Now then, raise her once more. Who'll make it four? Do I hear four? Three hundred once, three hundred twice—last call—and sold to—?

VOICE. Peter Wilkins, New Orleans.

SHORT. Mr. Wilkins, you've got a prize; please settle with the overseer. The next is a colored boy, commonly known as Rastus.

RASTUS. What's dat? Oh, massa, yo' gwine sell me? Please don't.

ESTA. Certainly, I am. I am tired of your nonsense; down the river you go.

SHORT. Now, gentlemen, here is a chance to secure a good body servant; sharp, active and a splendid worker.

RASTUS. Tell de trufe, massa Sho't man. I'se lazy as de debil, I'se hungry all de time and I ain't got sense. I'se foolish.

SHORT. What am I offered—who will start him?

VOICE. One dollar.

RASTUS. Yo' look hyar, massa, I ain't worf no dollar—bettah keep yo' dollar. Yo' don't want me. Oh, massa. don't send Rastus away; I'll be a good co'n-fiel' nigga ebery day.

ESTA. Well, I'll buy him in.

RASTUS. T'ank you massa. I tol' yo' niggers dey doan sell me; massa ain't gwine spar' me, I'se foolish.

SHORT. The next on the list is a little house servant, daughter of Uncle Jeff and Aunt Dinah. What do I hear?

Here AUNT DINAH *appears at door, and* UNCLE JEFF *enters* R. C. E.
Enter FLORENCE, R. I E. GARDNER *is well down* L. I E.

GARDNER. *(aside.)* Now is my chance to let her feel my power for evil. She may relent. It is expensive, but I will do it at any hazard.

SHORT. Here we have a likely child, six years of age and without mark or blemish. She was born on this plantation, and is the making of good nurse or servant. What do I hear?

VOICE. Fifty.

SHORT. Fifty dollars—very small bid, but it's a beginning. Now then, gentlemen from New Orleans, here is your chance. What do I hear? Bid up, bid up.

VOICE. One hundred.

FLOR. *(coming up stage.)* Two hundred.

ESTA. Florence, you are mad! What does this mean?

FLOR. It means that I have the allowance you gave me, and that if the additton to it of all my savings will accomplish it, I mean to save this child to her distresed mother.

ESTA. But I forbid this sentimental freak.

FLOR The money is mine, papa; you said I could do with it as I liked.

SHORT Excuse me; the sale must proceed. Two hundred—do I hear three? Who says three hundred?

GARDNER. *(aside.)* A chance for my revenge. Three hundred.

FLOR. Four humdred dollars.

GARDNER. Five.

FLOR. *(aside.)* I have but seven hundred dollars. If it goes higher, the child is lost. What shall I do?

SHORT. Five hundred I've heard, do I hear more? This is exciting—let us hear more. Who will bid again?

FLOR. Six hundred dollars.

GARDNER. Six fifty.

FLOR. Seven hundred—it is all I have. Papa, will you lend me more—I will repay you. Take my jewels or horse for security.

ESTA. No,—have done with this; you have compromised yourself and me enough already, by this folly.

SHORT. Seven hundred—do I hear more? Seven hundred dollars once, seven hundred twice—third and last—

GARDNER. Eight hundred dollars. *(aside.)* She is a little vixen, but I will conquer her.

SHORT. Eight hundred once—twice—third and last time—sold to Mr Gardner of Firdale Plantation, for eight hundred dollars. Well gentlemen, this closes the sale for the day, and the setlements are in order. If you will repair with me the little office of Mr. Estabrook,

beyond the mansion, we will close the transactions in regular shape.
                        (*Exit all except* FLORENCE *and* GARDNER.

FLOR.   Mr. Gardner, this is most ungenerous and unfair, but as
the little child is yours by purchase, I hope you will allow her to remain on your place, near her parents. Please keep her there, for
their sakes as well as for your own reputation for kindness.

GARDNER.   Miss Estabrook, you threw down the guantlet; you
met my advances with scorn and desired that we should be enemies.
Be it so.   I cannot be expected to waste sympathy upon the prote-
ges of one so bitterly disposed toward me.   The child goes down
the river.

FLOR. (*aside.*)   My intuitions were not at fault.   This man has
neither humane feeling or honor. (*to* GARDNER.) You are right, Mr.
Gardner, Florence Estabrook, though momentarily forgetful of it,
now appreciates the fact that her proper attitude toward a man of
your coarse and brutal instincts, is not one of supplicancy, but of de-
testation and scorn.   Your enmity does me honor, Mr Gardner.

CURTAIN.

ACT II.

SCENE I.—*Interior. - Sitting Room of* ESTABROOK'S *mansion , neatly
    furnished.   Tables, Chairs, Ornaments &c. tastily arranged.*
RASTUS *discovered dusting furniture and making a good pretense of
    being busy.*

RASTUS.   Dere yo' ol' furn'cher, yo' stan' still an' be wiped—
don't you go kickin' like young mule 'bout hyar.   I 'clar to goodness
I neber did see sech gwines on in all my black life.   Everybody
'pears like dey wus down in de mouf and 'tendin' funeral.   Sumfin's
gwine mighty wrong 'bout hyer, but I kaint help dat.   I'se a lucky
nigga not to git sol' and sent away, like dem good fer nuffin' smart
coons dat got sol' to-day.   Ef I hadn't tol' 'em I was foolish I'd bin a
goner, I reckon, and I'd a got some mastah what would a kep' me
in de field from mawnin' till night, and dat neber suit dis colored
gemman.   Take it all togedder, I'se glad I'se foolish.
              Enter DINAH, D. R., *carrying a tray.*
Dat you, Aunt Dinah; got somfin' for me to chaw on?   I'se gittin'
mighty hungry, I is.   Dat's me 'bout dis time.

DINAH.   No, Rastus, dis is fer de missus—poo' missus; she is
'bout done out wid de worry and 'eitement ob dis ebenin'.

RASTUS. I neber seed sech gwines on since I bin in dis house. I wonder what all dis is—

DINAH. 'Deed I don't know Rastus, but the place will neber seem to be de same to me or my ol' man. I neber t'ought dat massa Estabrook would sell any ob us, much leastwise my little Manda, dat I t'ought he liked.

RASTUS. Golly, but he wus powahful mad wid Miss Flo'ence fer her tryin' to buy Manda. I neber t'ink he would git so mad wid her, but she ain't skeered of him a bit. She jes' sed her say like as if she doan keer fo' nobody.

DINAH. But whar' is she now, Rastus?

RASTUS. I do' know; I do' know nuffin' 'cept I'se glad dey warn't gwine to buy me. When Manda wus sol' to Massa Gardner, Missy Flo'ence tol' me: Rastus get Tony; he and Frank are the only friends I have left; and wid de tears runnin' out'n dem eyes ob hers, she got on his back and galloped away, wid de dog follerin' her.

DINAH. I'se sorry she make massa mad for de sake of us black people, but I'll neber fuhgit how she tried to save my baby. Lo'd eber bress her pretty eyes fer dat; Dinah alwus lub her.

RASTUS. Yo' bettah git 'long wid missus' tea, or dey'll be sel-you next. Dey don't 'low no lazy niggers 'bout hyer.

DINAH. I'se gwine; but Rastus, did yo' heah what dey did wid Manda? Is dey gwine to take her 'way down to Orleans some whar?

RASTUS. I'se 'feard dey is, Aunt Dinah. Dat Gardner man is mad wid dese folks and I t'ink he's gwine ship Manda 'long wid de oders to New Orleans

DINAH. (taking up her tray.) And I'll neber see my baby agin'. Lo'd forgib eberybody, and dose dat took my Manda 'way f'm me.

(Exit in door L.

RASTUS. Po' Aunt Dinah, she has feelin's. I doan know 'bout losin' a chile, but golly, I feel awful tuff when massa wus gwine lose me; and dat Sho't man sed all he could to make 'em t'ink I'se smart nigger. Dat man's got ebil eye. I wus good min' ter git foolish 'n run 'way, but I'se skeered. Massa done tol' oberseer ter wboop me bad.

Enter SHORT at door R.

SHORT. Ah, there you are, my colored friend.

RASTUS. Massa Sho't man go 'way. I'se done 'fraid you's gwine sell me.

SHORT. But I want you.

RASTUS. I 'spec' you's got ter want. I'se got no truck wid yo'. I'se 'fraid ob you. I'se done hush my business.

SHORT. But, what's the matter, Sambo? You don't seem to like me.

RASTUS. I ain't no Sambo. I'se got my likes, and I doan like folks dat sell odder folks, no how

SHORT. Ah, you object to the auctioneer. Well, I am with you. After that scene to-day, I made up my mind to renounce the calling forever. Now Sambo

RASTUS. Rastus, Massa Sho't.

SHORT. I said Rastus, Sambo. I am looking for a red-handed murderer. Have you one about handy?

RASTUS. (*aside.*) Dar he go 'gin. I jus' reckon I run 'way 'fore he git wuss; he might want'r make a black-footed murderer out ob me. (*aloud.*) Yo' 'scuse me from furder talkin' Massa Sho't man, I'se gwine down ter git de ducks in be pen. (*Exit hastily.*

SHORT. That boy will never make a detective. Well, this has not been an uneventful day after all. Haughty father; spirited, yet feeling daughter, and designing lover have all appeared upon the scene, with the designing lover in the lead on the home stretch. By gracious, that girl is a wonder! How her eyes flashed as she bid against Gardner. If a look would kill, he would be a dead man this minute. She is the kind of girl I like. If ever A. Little Short embarks on the perilous voyage of matrimony, she is the kind of a girl he wants for his shipmate, and don't you forget to remember it.

FLOR. (*outside.*) All right, Rastus, tell them I have returned.

SHORT. Here she is now. If my heart keeps going up and down like this, I'll not be able to retain my equilibrium long enough to speak to her.

Enter FLORENCE, R. D.

Ah, good evening Miss Estabrook.

FLOR. Good evening, Mr. Short; excuse my unceremonious entrance; I thought all the visitors had departed.

SHORT. I think I am the last to linger. Your father wishes to consult me on a business matter, so I remained. I trust you will not blame me for anything displeasing in the incidents of this afternoon, Miss Estabrook; I only acted as I was compelled by my position, believe me.

FLOR. I do not blame you, Mr. Short; the whole affair was unfortunate and caused me much distress. The little one was my favorite, and I felt deeply for the parents.

SHORT. And that feeling does you credit, Miss Estabrook. Your struggle to relieve them, though unsuccessful, was heroic.

FLOR. I hope I was not unladylike.

SHORT. Indeed, no. You was earnest, yet womanly, and you

won the respect and admiration of every man present, save, possibly, one.

FLOR. You mean Mr. Gardner. It is just as well that I do not possess his esteem, as it would not honor me. His action to-day was contemptible, but I am confident that some day he will meet the just retribution his conduct deserves.

SHORT. I would like to take the job, with your permission.

FLOR. What!

SHORT. Just say the word, and like a knight of old, under your banner, and with your ribbon as a talisman, I will sally forth and make mince meat of this buyer of children.

FLOR. You are jesting.

SHORT. You know the proverb, many a truth is spoken in jest. What greater honor could be conferred on a man than to be chosen as your champion?

FLOR. You are very kind Mr. Short; but I have been used to being my own champion Should I require another, hower, I will not fail to remember your chivalrous offer.

SHORT. Do so, and you will always find me ready, metaphorically, to buckle on a sword in your behal.

FLOR. Thanks. How do you like our southern country, Mr. Short?

SHORT. It is charming, but less so than the daughters of the soil.

FLOR. You flatter.

SHORT. If truth be flattery, then I confess the soft impeachment. But, do you know, Miss Estabrock, I was afraid I would incur your displeasure by the position in which I was placed to day.

FLOR. But it is your business.

SHORT. That hardly justifies it. It has not always been my business and from this day henceforth I drop it. I never realized the horrors possible to the trafic in slaves and the disgrace in being a party to it, until I looked into your flashing eyes and saw you, against every obstacle, give battle for a little slave girl.

FLOR. But what will you do?

SHORT. I don't know—anything. I have been almost everything. from a lawyer's clerk to a cowboy on a ranch I have made a bit of everything; have traveled with everything, from a dramatic company to a threshing machine, and sold everything, from an elephant to a paper of needles. And yet I have nothing more subtantial to show for my erratic and versatile career than a lot of experience and a cheerful disposition.

FLOR   But will your desire for change ever be satisfied?

SHORT.   It is already.   When I look about me and realize how unprofitable my life has been, I long for a snug fireside and some one to care and struggle for beside myself.   But I fear I am boring you with this egotistical recital.   Turning to a pleasanter topic, Miss Estabrook, I know your fondnness for outdoor life, but what do you do on rainy days? .

FLOR.   I have my books and music.   Are you fond of music?

SHORT.   Very.   When at home I try to keep in contact and unison with the songs of the day.   Have you many?

FLOR.   (*bringing them to him.*)   Yes, here are some I got at New Orleans last winter.   Do you know any of them?

SHORT.   Nearly all; suppose we try them over.

FLOR.   With pleasure.   (*they sing.*)

Enter ESTABROOK *looking surprised.*

ESTA.   Well, Florence, I'm glad to see your spirits have improved since this afternoon, and you, Mr. Short, I did not know you were a singer?

SHORT.   My friends say I am not, my upper notes are decidedly weak,- but speaking of notes, how is the business getting on?

ESTA.   I have just finished with Mr. Brown, my overseer.   We had some difficulty in securing payment as we wanted it.   The sale has proved very remunerative. however, and I can meet my note with a little balance remaining.

SHORT.   But remember, it must leave by the mail packet tonight, to reach New Orleans before the expiration of the three days, grace.   What is the time now?

ESTA.   Nearly 8 o'clock.   The necessity for getting the money away to-night fairly slipped my mind; you know as a business man I am a decided failure.   What's to be done?   It's a good 7 miles to Roscoe and not a horse on the place could make it in time.

FLOR.   (*coming forward.*)   Yes there is papa—my Tony.

ESTA.   But no one can ride him but yourself

FLOR.   Then if it is an important mission, why cannot I be the messenger?

ESTA. *and* SHORT.   You!

FLOR.   Yes, I.   If I can ride about for pleasure why not for business.   Please papa let me go; I fear you are still angry with me for trying to buy little Manda but you will forgive me wont you, and to prove it let me do this mission for you.

SHORT.   It is the only chance Mr. Estabrook, but you are not afraid Miss Florence.

FLOR. I never was afraid of anything in my life; no one ever harmed me, so why should I be, besides have I not faithful friends, Tony and Frank, the fleetest horse and the smartest dog in the country round. Why I would feel as safe the darkest night as though I rode with a regiment of soldiers.

ESTA. Florence, child, this is a matter of the greatest importance or I would not have you risk it.

SHORT. Remember, it is your last hope.

ESTA. Then you may go. Short find Rastus and have him saddle Tony immediately. I will write a line to the brokers and enclose securities. Go, my child, and change your dress as quickly as possible and start at the earliest moment.

FLOR. Have no fear papa; the letter will reach Roscoe in time for the steamer or you may call Tony the slowest horse on the plantation.   (*Exit* R.

SHORT. What a wonderful girl; you should feel proud of her, Mr. Estabrook.

ESTA. I am. She is headstrong, fearless and impulsive. I must say I am pleased that she refused Gardner's addresses. I don't like the man--but hasten; tell Rastus to have the horse at the door at once if he values his black hide.

SHORT. Cool and bracing, I must say; the horse will be here or my name is not little Short.   (*Exit* L.

ESTA. Now, to write my letter and enclose money and securities. When it is in the mail pouch my mind will be at rest. (*Exit* R.

GARDNER. (*appears* D. L.) Luckily there was no one to announce me, otherwise I should not have known of the existing state of affairs and would have been unable to take a hand in it myself. My affairs are desperate; paying $800 for that damned nigger was a pretty piece of vengeance, but it has left me high and dry as far as money is concerned. This opportunity is too glorious to be lost. I can regain my money with a couple of thousand more, besides making that dare devil girl feel my power. My old friend in many a job of this kind is at Johnston tavern on the Roscoe road. He must do the work as he is unknown to her; now to get the start by 15 minutes. I'll arrange with him for the job, and then, revenge. She spurned my love, she called me a cur, and now she will feel my teeth.   (*Exit through window.*

SHORT. (*returning* L.) The horse will be here in a moment. Not here-- I knew the delay would not be caused by me.

Enter ESTABROOK *with large envelope in hand.*

ESTA. Here is the package secured and sealed. If it only reaches Roscoe before the boat leaves I will be a happy man, but where is Florence?

Enter FLORENCE *in riding habit.*

FLOR.　Here I am, papa.　Where is the package?

ESTA.　Here.　Be careful of it; if it be too late for the mail, take it to the landing and give it to the captain or first mate with instructions regarding its value.

RASTUS. (*coming in* L.)　Tony is ready, missy.

FLOR.　And so am I.

ESTA.　Be careful child; God keep you from harm, I feel as if something was going to happen.

FLOR.　Never fear for me papa, if Tony's speed is half as good as usual this letter will go down the river to night.

CHANGE.

SCENE II.　*Wood in* L.

Enter GARDNER *and* WOODRUFF.

GARDNER.　Quick, I say!　There is not a moment, a second to lose.　The greatest chance of our lives has presented itself, and we must not let it slip.

WOOD.　What is it now; tell me.　You dragged me away from a jolly crowd at Johnston's where I was enjoying myself--now what's in the wind?

GARDNER.　A great deal　Have you any means of disguising yourself and me?

WOOD.　From who—who are you afraid of?

GARDNER.　Afraid of no one, but I have a great scheme on foot. Florence Estabrook —

WOOD.　The gal you're in love with.　Wasn't the cold shake enough?　Are you still silly about her?

GARDNER.　Listen.　Her father has entrusted her with a valuable package of money and securities, that he says must reach Roscoe landing to-night.　As I am down to my last penny, the profits from our still have been little or nothing, and as $800 of my money is in that package I propose to get it back.

WOOD.　This is something like, but what is your scheme?

GARDNER.　Simple enough.　She is alone and unprotected. She does not know you, but you should have some disguise in case she sees you again.　My plan is to take money, girl and all.　It will be a secret revenge for the way she has insulted me.　We'll take her on to old Daddy Carey's place where my band of moonshiners have their headquarters, and the old man is my lieutenant. There we'll keep the fine lady, until she consents to become my wife.

The money will be yours but.Florence Estabrook will belong to me.

WOOD. Are your horses ready?

GARDNER. Yes I have ordered your's brought around. What have you for a disguise?

WOOD. Only these false beards. I was entertaining the party at Johnston's with reminiscences of their use--but where will we stop the gal.

GARDNER. I have thought of all that. By cutting across country and jumping a fence or two we can arrive at Johnston's Glen a good quarter of an hour before her. From there to Carey's is but a little ways. We can arrange further as we go along. Remember this job means more than money to me; it means revenge.

WOOD. You can have all the revenge you want, I take the money, I can do more with it.

GARDNER. Come on; the horses are waiting and we must ride as we never rode before. (WOODRUFF *crosses and exits at* L.) Florence Estabrook will be in my power in an hour. How I will gloat over her misery. But she shall not know who I am. At last I shall see this brave woman suing for mercy at my feet. (*Exit* L.

CHANGE.

SCENE III.—*Rocky pass in* 4. *Set Rocks. Roadway by river if practicable. Wild, desolate looking scene.*

Enter UNCLE JEFF, R. 4 E. *followed by* DINAH, *much fatigued.*

JEFF. (*speaking off.*) Come 'long mammy; don't lose yo' sperit; you's good for de balance ob de way in no time 'tall.

DINAH. 'Deed I'se putty nigh used up Dis day has bin nuffin but trouble and 'citement and dis yere ol' woman can't stand it.

JEFF. Jus' t'ink mammy, we'se gwine down to de landin' to hab de last last look at our Manda befo' dey take her away, p'raps foreber.

DINAH. I know; but let me res' my old bones a minit, and den I'll be as spry as a June bug. Unc' Jeff, I must res' jus' a minit.

JEFF. All right, Dinah. I guess we got time ter make de landin'. By crossin' tru de bresh an' climin' ober de rocks, we save a good mile. How yo' feel now, Dinah?

DINAH. Jus' tol'ble--look yer. I can't git it tru my black wool why Mars' Ga'dner took sech a powa'ful shine to our Manda. He mus' set a heap on her when pay all dat money fo' her.

JEFF. I doan t'ink it's dat. 'Pears to me ders's trouble 'twixt him an' little missy. Lo'd bress her, how she did stan' up an' sass eberybody for our little gal. 'Deed I'll neber fo'git her fo' dis day's work.

DINAH. She's de sweetest flowah dat eber grew in dis worl' I done t'ought Mars Ga'dner would keep de chile hyar, but he took 'tickler pains dat no one should talk to her 'til she was handed ober to de spec'later.

JEFF. An' it was him dat sed dat we could bid Manda good-bye at de landin'.

DINAH. 'Deed I'm disappinted in Massa Estabrook. Neber did I t'ink he would sell any ob his people.

JEFF. Doan say nuffin' 'gin de massa. Maybe it wus all fo' de bes'. De good Lo'd may hab some good objec' in takin' her—but come, Dinah, we mus' be gwine. *(helps her up, and they move slowly down* L. 1 E.

Enter GARDNER *and* WOODRUFF, R. U. E., *unperceived.*

GARDNER. Here we are; this is the place and we are in time.

WOOD. Hush! Who are them people? I thought you said the place was deserted.

GARDNER. A couple of niggers going home, I take it—listen.

JEFF. Now ol' lady, stir yo' stumps; jus' put yo' bes' foot to de front and we'll be at de landin' in free shakes ob a dead lamb's tail.

DINAH. All right, Jeff, I'm a comin'.

GARDNER. *(to* WOODRUFF.) The effectual way to dispose of these people is to frighten them. You know how superstitious they are? Just watch— *(both hide behind rock.)*

GARDNER. *(sighing profoundly.)* Ah!

WOOD. Ah!

DINAH. *(turning quickly.)* Jefferson Washin'ton Estabrook! What wus dat noise?

JEFF. Go on, ol' woman. Dey wasn't no noise—yo'se gittin' silly.

GARDNER. Ah!

WOOD. Ah!

JEFF Dinah Marfa Sophronia Estabrook, I done heerd de noise dat time. What yo' reckon 'tis.

DINAH. Oh, I'se silly, but I 'spec it's spooks, 'n I wish I wus home.

JEFF. *(much frightened.)* Spooks! Doan be skeered. Look at me. *(trembling.)* I'se cool as cowcumber. *(wiping face with bandana.)* Dere ain't no sech t'ing as spooks.

GARDNER. *(with deep voice.)* Who is it that dares to come into the Hoodoo camp? They must die.

JEFF *and* DINAH *(clinging together.)* Oh, I wish I wus home.

GARDNER. Ah!

JEFF. Ah! 'Scuse me massa Hoodoo, I ain't got no business hyer. I'se gwine right away! Come 'long yo' foolish ol' woman; yo' done cause all dis 'sturbance.

GARD. *and* WOOD. Ah!

JEFF. (*shoving* DINAH *off.*) Ah, yo'se'f 'n see how yo' like it.

(*Exit*, L. 1. E.

GARDNER. (*coming down.*) I think we have disposed of them. There's no danger of interruption from that quarter. But now to business—is everything perfectly understood?

WOOD. Yes; I have a horse and buggy about twenty rods from here. Will you take her horse?

GARDNAR I think it best that we leave her horse behind. It will look more like a mysterious disappearance. to have it found wandering about. Besides, it might be recognized with us.

WOOD. This has been hurried work—but we have arrived on time.

GARDNER. None too soon. I hear the canter of a horse now-quick, my disguise, and mind I must keep, well in the background. I don't want her to recognize me yet. When you have her in the buggy, I will start for home and so avert suspicion, and you meet me at Daddy Carey's as we agreed.

WOOD. Leave her to me. She's not the first I have brought to terms. But listen, be ready. She is here. (*Music. Horses hoofs heard outside.*)

Enter FLORENCE R. U. E. *followed by Frank.*

(WOODRUFF *and* GARDNER *hide behind the rocks. As* FLORENCE *appears,* WOODRUFF *rushes out, and seizes horse's bridle.*)

WOOD. Just stop a moment, please.

FLOR. How dare you stop my horse. Release his bridle at once.

Wood. Not so fast, Miss. This is no time of night for a young woman to be galloping about in dangerous places. You need a protector.

FLOR. You are insulting. Release my horse's head this instant or you will bitterly repent this insolence.

WOOD. Still fiery. Then I must come to the point at once. I'll trouble you for a package you are carrying to Roscoe Landing.

FLOR. Package? What package? I have no package.

WOOD. I am sorry to be discourteous to a lady, but you are telling a falsehood. Enough of this nonsense—so out with it—the money I must have.

FLOR. What I told you was not true. I have a package which

I have been commissioned by my father to deliver at Roscoe to-night. It is a sacred trust, and I will fulfil it at all hazards. (*drawing revolver.*) Come and take it at your peril.

WOOD. (*releasing horse for a moment.* You she devil!

GARDNER. (*rushing from behind rock.*) Don't let her escape.

FLOR. (*as* WOODRUFF *wrests revolver from her.*) Heaven protect me.

WOOD. Now, my fine lady, the tables are turned. Quick! off that horse, or I'll spoil that pretty face of yours. Here Jim, (*to* GARDNER,) fasten the horse and let's be off.

FLOR. I beg of you, if you have any manhood or compassion in your hearts, do not keep me from the performance of my duty. Delay means the ruin and disgrace of my father. Surely he nor I have ever wronged you; why should do such a cowardly thing as to rob me and mine.

WOOD. Little mercy you would show us at the muzzle of your pistol, you wild cat. No, we are determined--the money we must have.

FLOR. (*taking off medallion.*) If you want money, here, take this. It is very valuable--a present from my father; but do not rob me of my trust.

WOOD. (*snatching the jewel.* Your'e a fool! We'll have this as well. Here, Jim, take this trinket and take care of it. (*hands jewel to* GARDNER, *who places it in an envelope and puts it in his overcoat pocket.*) Now for the package, quick!

FLOR. You shall not have it; I'll die first.

GARDNER. (*aside to* WOODRUFF.) Don't be rough. Easy with her until you get to Carey's--then you can get it.

WOOD. As you say—but I'd like to strangle the little spit-fire. You look out for the dog. Come Miss. You must come with me this way.

FLOR. I will not.

WOOD. It's no use we must use force. (GARDNER *throws a cape over her head from behind.*) See, we have you at last. (FLORENCE *resists, but finally gives up. The dog attacks* GARDNER.)

(*Exit* GARDNER *and dog* R. 2. E., *struggling.*

WOOD. Now to administer a little quieting medicine. She will hardly return to consciousness before our journey's end. (*Puts phial to her nostrils.*) Gardner seems to be having trouble with that brute. The best way to settle him would be a bullet from this pistol. But no—the shot might give the alarm. It's better to be on the safe side. (*Enter* GARDNER *looking used up.*) Well, is he all right?

GARDNER. Yes, but after a terrible struggle. The beast seemed to realize that he was fighting for his mistress and gave me· an awful battle.

WOOD. Your hand is bleeding, did he bite you?

GARDNER. Yes. This handkerchief will stop the flow--it's nothing dangerous. I have him safely tied to a tree; he can do no further harm. What about the girl?

WOOD. She's quiet enough, and liable to remain so. Lend a hand and we'll be off and in a short time we'll be safe in Carey's den.

GARDNER. The girl and the money both secured with little difficulty; this is a glorious night's work. And now Miss Estabrook, you bid fair to become the moonshiner's bride. Come.

(Exit L. 2. E., carrying FLORENCE between them.

As they go off, the dog appears with rope dragging, the end frayed, as if bitten off. He looks after them and then unties the horse and leads him off.

CURTAIN.

.... ____ ____

ACT III.

SCENE I. -*Interior of kitchen. Door and window at back.*

DINAH *discovered washing dishes etc.*

DINAH. Dis don't seem like de happy mawnin' we done hab here ever since I belong to Massa Estabrook. Everything seems gwine wrong and all de niggers look skeerd to death. Dat was such a 'sprise to dem yisterd'y dat dey don't know what to 'spect next. Well dis is de worst dey could do to me ard Jeff; took 'way our little Manda; after dat dere's no trubble can grieve our hearts 'cept dey'd part me and my ol' man, and I reckon Massa wouldn't do dat.

Enter UNCLE JEFF *hurriedly* D. F.

JEFF. Dinah! Dinah! did yo' hear de news— did yo' hear it?

DINAH. What's de mattah wid yo' man- what news you 'spect I ha'r?

JEFF. 'Bout Missy Florence-

DINAH. Missy Florence? Why I 'spose she's 'way for her mo'nin' ride—de plantation don't see much ob little Missy dis time ob day.

JEFF. But ain't yo' hea'd? She aint been home all de night, and de Massa and ol' Missy are nigh crazy 'bout it.

DINAH. Why, when did she go?

JEFF. Last night—but hyar comes Rastus. He may bring good news.

Enter RASTUS *door in flat.*

RASTUS. What yo' lazy niggers doin' hyar? Why ain't yo' out lookin' for little Missy?

DINAH. I jes heerd she was done gone, from Unc' Jeff. But Rastus, tell us all 'bout it.

RASTUS. Well. I ain' got no time to flitter 'way wid yo' common niggers, but if Aunt Dinah has just a drap ob sperits what she puts in her puddin', I might be able to tell yo' all 'bout it.

DINAH. (*bringing bottle and glass.*) Here Rastus—now tell us. I'm all in a fluster—how did it happen, and where do dey t'ink she is?

RASTUS. (*taking drink.*) Dat's jes like you women you'se always askin' questions, moah questions in a minit dan a man can answer in a week. (*takes another drink.*) Why don't yo' take it cool like I do?

JEFF. Go on Rastus—tell us what yo' know.

RASTUS. Well since you're so pressin'—it's jes dis way—yo' see frum what I could h'ar tru de key holes and 'round the corners, ol' Massa done owed some money what had to be paid 'mediately if not sooner—and dat am de reason all de little ones was sold yisterd'y.

DINAH. Yes, and our poor Manda 'mong 'em.

RASTUS. De ol' man feel awful bad 'bout it, but it couldn't be helped, he had to hab de money. Well it seems dat de money had to go down to Orleans on de packet last night, and dey didn't find it out till de las' minit; den de Massa called me and asked my advice. He say to me, "Rastus, how I get dat money down to de boat;" den I say to him, Massa, dere's only one horse dat can make dat journey in time, and dat's Tony. Den he says to me, who can ride de horse, and Missy Florence says, I'll take it, and sho' 'nough, dat gal got on de horse, dat I brought 'round to de door—and galloped 'way into de darkness ob de night, and we hain't seen her since. Ol' Massa don't know what become ob her—or wheder somt'ing happen to her on de way home.

JEFF. Why she wasn't at de landin' when de boat started.

RASTUS. How yo' know dat, man?

DINAH. Yo' be careful Jeff; if dey know yo'd left de plantation las' night, yo'd get de whippin' post.

RASTUS. Look heah—if yo' niggers know anything 'bout dat boat—or dat landin', you jes tell de Massa. He won't hab you harmed, he bress you. I'll go bring him heah, and yo' speak de truf, de whole truf—and nothing but de truf, so help yo' bob. (*Exit* L. 2 E.

DINAH. Now yo' see what yo' done, got yo'se'f in trubble, for talkin' too much. Dey say de women are always gettin' into trubble wid dere tongues—but ebery time a man opens his mouf, he puts his foot in it.

JEFF. Never mind Dinah—if I does get a beatin' I'll tell de Massa what I know, and saw at de landin'. It may ease his mind 'bout Little Missy.

DINAH. Yes, when he heahs we bof broke de rule 'bout gwine off the place at night, den we bof get whipped.

JEFF. No, indeed, Dinah, de ol' Massa feels de sorrow ob his own child's loss now, too much to make us poor colored people suffer more.

(*Enter* ESTABROOK *followed by* RASTUS *door* R. 2 E.

ESTA. What's this I hear, Jeff? Rastus tells me you were at Roscoe Landing last night?

JEFF. Yes, massa Estabrook, I hope yo' fo'gib me fo' breakin' de rule, but dat wus de las' chance we had to see our little Manda 'fore she wus taken away; so we walk 'cross de woods an' seed her fo' de las' time.

ESTA. How long were you there before the boat started?

JEFF. 'Bout ten minutes, sah.

ESTA. And all that time you stood so that you could see any one that rode up to the landing?

JEFF. Yes sah; right by de gang plank.

ESTA. And did my daughter, Miss Florence, ride up there while you were waiting?

JEFF. No, sah.

ESTA. Are you sure?

JEFF. Yes, sah; and she wusn't dar befo' dat, 'caze somebody would a seed her an' tol' 'bout it.

ESTA. True, true—my worst fears seem to be realized. She must have been stopped on the road to the landing and robbed, perhaps murdered.

RASTUS. (*aside.*) I belebe it wus dat Sho't man—he's allers talkin' 'bout murder. Golly! speak ob de debil 'n he's sho' to turn up.

Enter SHORT,—D. F.

SHORT. Ah, here you are, Mr. Estabrook. I have been looking for you everywhere.

ESTA. For God's sake, speak—any trace of her?

SHORT. Not the slightest. We have gone over every inch of ground between here and Roscoe Landing since daybreak. There is not the slightest trace of any struggle.

RASTUS. Den I done bettah dan yo' Mr. Sho't. I done found suffin' dis mawnin'.

SHORT. What was it, Rastus?

RASTUS. (*producing a piece of rope.*) Dis'yer. I foun' it 'bout twenty feet f'om de road, tied to a tree. Now rope doan grow on no trees, so I ontied de todder en' 'n t'ought I bring it 'long hyar.

SHORT. Rastus, your keen, observing faculties will promote you to the detective force yet. This is our first clue. Did the earth about the tree look as if there had been a scuffle?

RASTUS. Yes sah, it was toah up like.

SHORT. Ah, I see it all; we have struck the right trail at last. If you notice, this end of the rope has been bitten off, doubtless the work of some animal, and probably of your sagacious four-footed friend, Frank. He tried to help his mistress and was tied up for his pranks, but Rastus where did you find this rope?

RASTUS. At a place dat we folks about hyar call Johnston's Glen.

JEFF. (*to* DINAH.) Why dat's where we heerd de spooks.

SHORT. What's that?

ESTA. I neglected to tell you Mr. Short, that these colored people were at the landing when the boat started, and up to that time Florence had not arrived.

SHORT. What was that they said about spooks?

DINAH. It wasn't me, Mr. Short, it was dat man of mine. I didn't say nuffin'.

JEFF. Yes—but yo' said suffin when you heerd dat spook go ah!

DINAH. Deed, I didn't want to say nuffin'—I want to scoot

SHORT. But where did all this happen?

JEFF. Near dat place Rastus am talkin' 'bout, Johnston's Glen.

SHORT. Tell me all about it? (*to* ESTABROOK.) This may lead to something.

JEFF. Well sah, yo' see me and Dinah, here—we wanted to git a las' look at our Manda, what yo' sol' yisterd'y, and so afteh da'k we sta'ted fo' de landin'. When we got to Johston's Glen by de sho't cut, Dinah hear, who is gittin' ol'—

DINAH. Ol, yo'se'f; I'm twice es spry es yo' is now.

JEFF. W'y Dinah, yo'se good five yeahs ol'er dan me.

DINAH. Heah dat fool nigger—yo' go long. I'se nuffin' but a young gal now.

RASTUS. Yes yo'se bof ol' 'nuff ter eat hay.

ESTA. Rastus be quiet. Go on, Jeff.

JEFF. Well, sah, Dinah want to sit down an' res' herse'f, so down she sot. Jus' as we gwine on, she heerd a voice sayin' –Ah! and golly, if it did'n' skeer me mos' to de'f.

SHORT. Did it say anything more?

JEFF. Yes sah, it said ef we didn't git 'way fom dat dar place de hoodoo would foller us all our lives. So we git out ob dar quick.

SHORT. (*to* ESTA.) Ah, the returns are coming in. Doubtless this robbery or abduction was planned, and as the presence of these negroes about the place interfered with its execution, they were frightened away.

ESTA. But how could they have planned the robbery; no one knew of the arrangment for remitting the money except you and I.

SHORT. That is a mystery that we must unravel. But, at least, we are on the track. Come, let us look over the ground again. A thorough examination of this Johnston Glen may enable us to get on the trail of the abductors.

ESTA. If you will join me in the library in a few minutes, I will accompany you. I must tell Mrs. Estabrook that we have a clue, though a faint one. (*Exit*, R. 3. E.

SHORT. Sambo, allow me to congratulate you. You are the hero of the hour; to you we owe our thanks for the first clue.

RASTUS. Yo' doan owe Rastus nuffin'. I done heerd what massa say. Dere wus only free dat know dat little missy had de money, an' was gwine carry it to de landin'. De, is Massa Estabrook. Mistah Sho't and Rastus Now it wusn't Massa Estabrook what stole de gal and de money, and it wusn't Rastus, and dere s only one odder person what know'd; so dar yo' is, Mistah Sho't.

SHORT. What do you mean?

RASTUS. I'se got my meanin'.

SHORT. Do you mean to say that I stole the money and carried off Miss Florence?

RASTUS. Oh, I ain't sayin' nuffin'; I'se foolish.

SHORT. Why, you black scoundrel, I have a great mind to throw you out of the window

RASTUS. No sah, doan do dat. Dere's a big watch troff under dat windeh, an' I might spile de watch.

SHORT. Then the water must be spoiled --

Siezes RASTUS, *from under whose clothes fall to the floor cakes, cookies and a pie, seeing which,* DINAH *comes to* SHORT'S *assistance and together they pitch* RASTUS *out of the window. Splash.*

RASTUS. (*at window, dripping.*) Better not do dat 'gin. I'se foolish. [CHANGE.]

SCENE II.—*Plain Chamber in* L.

Enter MRS. ESTABROOK, L. I. E.

MRS. ESTA.   What a night of misery I have passed, doubt and anxiety regarding the fate of my little one has nearly driven me frantic.   It seems an age since yesterday; sorrow indeed lengthens one's hours.

Enter ESTABROOK R. I. E.

My dear husband, tell me, tell me quickly has anything been heard of our darling child?

ESTA.   We have found a slight clue, but so slight that I fear to base much hope upon it.

MRS. ESTA.   And that is—?

ESTA.   A piece of rope has been found tied to a tree one end of which has been gnawed off.   Our friend Short has a theory that when Florence was attacked, her dog Frank tried to save her, but was tied up and subsequently escaped.

MRS. ESTA.   But how could you, her father, send her out into the night on such a journey?

ESTA.   Do not reproach me my dear wife, my cup of misery is already full.   Her words yesterday when interceding for little Manda, are ever present in my mind.   It seems prophetic, for she said: "If you inflict this great wrong upon your servants, some of your loved ones may be taken from you, and you be made to feel the torture of a more painful separation."   How soon have her words been realized.

MRS. ESTA.   Bear up Hiram.   We must not lose hope, and should our daughter be restored to us, we should try to buy back little Manda, for I feel with you, that this is a punishment inflicted upon us for separating a child from its parents.

ESTA.   This has been a fearful lesson to me.   As Heaven is my witness, I'll never sell another slave as long as I live.

Enter GARDNER R. I E.

GARDNER.   Good morning, Mr. Estabrook, good morning, Mrs. Estabrook—you will pardon my entering unannounced, but the house seems in such a confusion that there was no one to announce me.

ESTA.   We have suffered a terrible loss, Mr. Gardner.

GARDNER.   Yes, I have heard, and wished to be the first to express my sympathy and to do all in my power to help you in your search.

ESTA.   I thank you, Mr. Gardner.   You must excuse my hasty words of yesterday.   I was very much annoyed, and must confess I doubted your friendship.   Your hearty tender of help in this our extremity, convinces me that I wronged you.

GARDNER. You did, indeed. I love your daughter sincerely, but as she does not reciprocate my feelings, I have tried to think it may be for the best. I was too hasty in my words to her, but now that she may be in imminent peril, we must do everything in our power to find and restore her to her mother's arms.

MRS. ESTA. I thank you, Mr. Gardner. This is the greatest sorrow of my life. My poor dear; I am distracted when I think of her possible fate. Please excuse me— (*Exit*, L. 1. E.

GARDNER. Poor woman, her heart is nearly broken. Indeed, Mr. Estabrook, your wife and you have my heartfelt sympathy— but something must be done, and at once. I cannot understand how anything could have happened of a serious nature. She is a perect horsewoman and knows the country well. Again, what object could any one have had in molesting her?

ESTA. Robbery, I fear.

GARDNER. Robbery?

ESTA. Yes. I foolishly allowed her to be the bearer of a large sum of money to Roscoe Landing. It was necessary that it should be there last night before the departure of the south bound packet. She volunteered to be the messenger and I, fearing no danger, consented. It will be a lifelong regret to me, and should she not be found it will kill her mother.

GARDNER. She had a sum of money with her?

ESTA. Yes, the proceeds of the sale of yesterday.

GARDNER. That puts a new face upon the affair.

ESTA. Why? What do you mean?

GARDNER. That her disappearance may have been voluntary.

ESTA. I do not understand you.

GARDNER. Mr. Estabrook, I appreciate your feelings as a father and dislike to give exression to a theory of your daughter's absence that may wound you deeply.

ESTA. Speak, man; do not keep me in suspense.

GARDNER. As you know, I love Miss Florence and would make her my wife, but the circumstances of this affair lead me to suspect that she was not abducted, but has run away.

ESTA. Mr. Gardner, how dare you say such a thing regarding my daughter. Were I not an old man, sir, I would crush you to the earth.

GARDNER. Easy, Mr. Estabrook. I knew I would offend you, but it is just as well to face all the possibilities. Your daughter is wild, imperious, and headstrong. You thwarted her in a matter upon which she had set her heart, and she is impatient of restraint. Do you remember her words when she wished you to spare the child? "Papa," she said, "you will regret this to the last day of your life."

ESTA.   It is true; but I cannot harbor such a thought.   My child upon whom I have lavished affection, whose happiness has been my sole object in life, she to be so ungrateful?   No. I will not believe it. She may be wild, she may be headstrong, but Florence Estabrook is not a thief.

GARDNER.   There you misunderstand me.   I would not insinuate that she had stolen the money, but could she not have visited some of her friends, could she not have purposely stayed away last night, to punish you for your imagined cruelty to her?   Is not my theory reasonable?

ESTA.   It is not only unreasonable, but it is unjust.

GARDNER.   Believe me Mr. Estabrook, I am sorry that I gave words to my thoughts.   I hope you do not think the less of me for so doing?

ESTA.   I understand you perfectly Mr. Gardner, but it is evident you do not understand the girl whom you would make your wife.

GARDNER.   Then to show my interest in her welfare, I ask to be employed in a renewal of the search.   We will leave no foot of the ground between here and Roscoe unexplored.   Something is likely to result from our search.

Enter SHORT, hurriedly.

SHORT.   Ah, here you are, Mr. Estabrook.   We have examined the ground near where the knawed rope was found, and there are signs of a struggle having occurred there.   But there the clue ends as yet; no trail of people going in any direction, was discovered. Now, we must organize parties to go in different directions from that point as a centre, and scour the country for twenty miles around.

GARDNER.   Yes, that is a good suggestion, Mr. Estabrook; and lest you should imagine that I am inflexibly wedded to my own theory, I offer to take charge of one of the parties.

ESTA.   Thank you, Mr. Gardner, I believe you are sincere.

SHORT. (*aside.*)   And I believe he is a damned rascal.

ESTA.   But come, let us start at once.   There is not a moment to be lost.   (*Exit, R. 1. E.*

GARDNER. (*aside.*)   My plan is succeeding admirably.   I will follow the right trail, send them in other directions, and thus throw them completely off the scent.   (*Exit R. 1 E.*

SHORT.   If I'm any judge of human nature, that man is a scoundrel.   I don't know why I say so, but I am compelled to.   His actions yesterday do not lead me to infer that he will do much for the fare of Miss Florence. I may be mistaken, but I'll gamble a twenty-dollar gold piece to a stick of candy that I am not. My fine Southern gentleman I'll keep my weather eye on you, and if you're in any way tricky I'll be down on you like a thousand of brick. (*Exit* R. I E.

. . . .

SCENE III.--*Carey's Den. A tumble-down place. Door* R. C. *Window* L. C. *Another door with bars across*, L. 3. E.

As scene draws off a crowd of rough men discovered seated on benches, drinking from tin cups; some playing cards. CAREY *dozing by fireplace*, R. 2. E. MOTHER CAREY, *an old hag is quieting men, who are laughing loudly.*

MOTHER C. Hush, hush my pretty birds, or you'll waken the old man, and some of you will find he's not in a cheerful humor. Something has gone wrong at the still, and he's as cross as two sticks.

VOICE. All right mother, but give us some more liquor.

MOTHER C. Ah, that's what you want my pretty birds, ah, you take to it as a duck does to water.

ALL. (*loudly.*) Drink fair, and give us some more.

CAREY. (*waking.*) What's all this noise? What do you all mean by raising such a row; do you think you are in a tavern? And you, you old fool, is that the way to keep them quiet, filling them up with drink? The first thing you know the officers will be down upon us, and the whole concern will be snuffed out and we in limbo.

MOTHER C. I only just give 'em a bit, 'deed I did.

ALL. That's so--that's so--

CAREY. Be quiet! all of you. I,ve had bad news, to-day, and we've got to be very shady, instead of taking more chances.

MOTHER C. What is it, Daddy?

ALL. Yes, what is it—tell us?

CAREY. Well, the revenue officers have had some hint of our place here. I don't know if we have a traitor among us, but if we have, he's got to die. You remember your oath?

ALL. We do.

CAREY. Then think of it well. You know me and your captain. The man who splits on us will take his life in his hands. So take heed.

MOTHER C. Don't be harsh, Daddy; the boys are all good fellers, and not a telltale or coward amongst 'em.

ALL. Good for the old woman— hurrah!

CAREY.   Hush!   Be quiet, curse you.   If suspicion is once directed to our den, we'll have to make tracks on short notice; so we'll have to keep quiet for the sake of our necks.   Keep watch of every stranger and let no one approach if at all suspicious. (*whistle outside*) Hush! what's that. (*whistle repeated.*) Quick! clear the cabin.   Your voices were heard, and perhaps they're down on us already.   Out with you quietly, by the back way, and make for the cave near Watson's Bluff.   Quick! (*knock on the door.   Exit the gang.*) Old woman you go to the door. (*sits by the fire, pretending sleep.*

MOTHER. C. (*goes to door, opens it a little.*) Who's there?

WOOD. (*outside.*)   Hurry up, open the door.

MOTHER C. (*in a trembling voice.*)   I don't know you.   We're afraid; me and my old man are scared of robbers.   You can't come in here.

WOOD. (*loudly.*)   Open the door I say, and be quick.   Tell Daddy Carey I'm from the Captain.

CAREY. (*coming to door.*)   And he told you to tell me —

WOOD.   The moon is out to-night.

CAREY.   It's all right, let him in,   I hope the Captain is not taking chances? (MOTHER CAREY *opens door,* WOODRUFF *enters carrying* FLORENCE, *he places her in chair.*)

WOOD.   I thought you'd never let me in.

MOTHER C.   What is this you've got?   A lady--who is she?

WOOD.   Never mind that now; give me a drop of liquor to revive her.   We've had a long hard ride, and she's not in the best of conditions.   Hurry up, give me some whisky.

CAREY.   I don't like the looks of this.   My place is in rather bad repute now, and this job won't help matters.

WOOD.   Well, I came here by the Captain's orders.   He said bring her here, and here she is

CAREY.   But what's to be done with her?   This is no place to keep a woman.

WOOD.   Well, that's his affair.   Put her in a good safe place; its only for to-morrow and then he takes her to a place that is being prepared for her.

CAREY.   Well, its lucky I started the boys to the mountain.   It won't do to have too many witnesses to a job like this.   From her dress she's a lady, and there'll be a search the whole country round.   Probably a big reward.   The Captain is growing too bold, I've told him that women would be his downfall, and darn me if he hasn't started in that track already.   (FLORENCE *moans.*)

WOOD.   There, she is coming to, where can we put her?

CAREY. (*pointing* L.) In there; we call it the guard room ,and sometimes lock some of the boys up if they get refractory.

MOTHER C. Oh, don't put her in there; she's such a little woman, and she looks all tired out.

CAREY. There you go again with your whining. Don't be a tender-hearted fool; this is no job of ours, and the sooner its over the better.

WOOD. We had trouble enough. Perhaps the old woman can coax her better than we can, she's a plucky woman, and a little she-devil when aroused. Let us leave her with Mother Carey.

CAREY. Perhaps it's best. We'll go to the stables and see that your horse is put away. I'll lock the door on the outside, so there'll be no chance for her to escape—come. (*Exit* WOODRUFF, D. F., *locking the door.*)

MOTHER CAREY. (*approaching* FLORENCE.) Poor thing, I feel sorry for her; but it would be worth my life to try to help her. Here little lady, bear up, open your eyes and drink this. (*Puts cup to her lips.*) Ther's a goods little lady; yes, she's coming to—poor thing, she has fallen into hard hands. The Captain has no mercy and will bind her to his will, if he so chooses. (*Steps to fire-place sits down.*)

FLOR. (*slowly revives and looks about her.*) Where am I? What does all this mean? Is this a horrible dream from which I will awaken? Oh, it is too dreadful to be reality. (*sees* MOTHER C.) Speak to me; who and what are you, and why am I here?

MOTHER C. (*comes to her.*) Be quiet, little girl, you're all right. Keep still and you'll be treated well, but if you scream or raise a row you are among people who will stop your voice in a way that won't be pleasant. (*goes to door* L. 2. E. *unlocks it*)

FLOR. What dreadful plot is this? I seem to have been in a dream—oh I remember, now, those men in the woods tried to take the package, but it here, safe in my bosom; they have not taken it from me. I see it all; they have brought me here to rob, perhaps murder me. Merciful heaven, what shall I do, which way shall I turn? (*staggers to door, tries it.*) It is locked—perhaps this way; oh, I must escape. (*Meets* MOTHER CAREY, *who is returning.*)

MOTHER C. Don't hurry in there; you'll be in soon enough, and once in that room, it's a hard job to get out.

FLOR. Let me go. Please let me go. You must have some feeling in your heart for a weak defenceless woman. On my knees I beg that you will open that door and let me go.

MOTHER C. Little one, I feel for you, but I am as helpless as yourself. You are in the power of a cruel villian who rules us all here with an iron hand. I cannot help you, but let me advise you, let me give you some nourishment, it will give you strength. and will fit you for a struggle in case you have a chance to escape. I would be your friend, for your sweet face and your suffering touches my heart; but I cannot help you, as God is my judge.

FLOR. But what is this place, where am I? Who are the people who live here?

CAREY. (*heard outside*.) Everything is all right, look out for the step.

MOTHER C. Quick! they are returning; go in there and be as brave as you can. I will get you something to eat, and will help you if I can.

FLOR. I will trust you, God bless you for your words.

(*Exit* D. L. 2 E.

Re-enter WOOD *and* CAREY.

WOOD. Then you think the revenue officers have suspected this place?

CAREY. Nothing certain, but I believe in being a ware hawk. When strangers are about, keep close has been my motto, and if they get too inquisitive, there's always a way to satisfy their curiosity.

WOOD. You mean by

CAREY. Never mind what I mean, you understand, don't give it words.

WOOD. You've such a tender way of speaking that you send cold chills down my back. Here, Mother Carey, give me a drink of the mountain dew to raise my spirits.

MOTHER C. (*getting liquor*.) Don't mind him; he don't mean half he says. His heart's all right.

CAREY. You keep a quiet tongue in your head, or that will not be all right. Where's the girl?

MOTHER C. She's safe enough. Where no one can break in and steal her.

WOOD. Curse her, I wish some one would. This is a sort of job that I don't like. I never fought with a woman before, and this one has nearly been my match. (*whistle heard outside. All start.— Whistle repeated.* CAREY *extinguishes light*.)

CAREY. Hush!--don't move (*knock at door*.)

GARDNER. (*outside*.) The moon is out to-night.

WOOD. It's the captain's voice.

GARDNER. (*outside*.) Open the door; I am in great haste.

CAREY. (*unfastening the door*.) Come in, Captain, come in.

Enter GARDNER.

GARDNER. Quick! I haven't a moment to spare. (*to* WOOD.) So you're here all right; that's good. Did you have any trouble with her?

WOOD. She fought like a wild cat, and only gave in when I gave her another dose of the chloroform. It did not hurt her though for she is as lively as ever, now.

GARDNER. Where is she?

CAREY. In that room. It is a secret prison I have for fractious members of our band. Unless you knew it was there, it would be a hard task to find it.

. GARDNER. (*to* WOOD.) Did you get the money from her? (*at the word, "money"* MOTHER CAREY, *who sits by the fire, looks up.*

CAREY. So there's money in this job, Captain. I thought you weren't taking long odds for love alone; you're heart ain't so tender as all that.

GARDNER. It's love, revenge and money, Carey, and you needn't fear but that you shall have your share of the plunder. This plan was as hastily as daringly conceived. This woman has spurned my love, but her hatred has only made me the more determined to possess her.

WOOD. But what is your plan?

GARDNER. It is to instruct you regarding that, that I am here. After leaving you, I hastened home, was seen by everyone, to be able to prove an alibi. In the morning I rode over to Estabrook's, and was just in time to express my sympathy to my future father-in-law, and to show him my burning anxiety to find the darling of his heart. I undertook to lead one of the searching parties, and insisted on coming this way knowing this part of the country very well. I sent my followers on a wild goose chase, and come here to find how all had progressed.

WOOD. Well, now that she is here, what is next to be done?

GARDNER. Give us onother drink, Mother Carey, and take your pay out of this. (*throws her a bill.*) Well, the first thing is to get the money. This must be accomplished at once. Remember, Woodruff, that it it is to be yours, save a portion for our honest friend Daddy Carey.

CAREY. Yes, times are very hard, and it's all I can do to keep the wolf from the door.

WOOD. That's all right Daddy, the wolf that comes to your door would stand a good chance of getting the worst of it himself.

GARDNER. Enough of this jesting. You, Woodruff, give her another dose of that sleep producer and with Mother Carey's assistance get the package from her. Then push on at once to Redding's crossing on the river, go to the tavern, pay liberally, and they'll ask no questions. Keep her under lock and key, and day after to-morrow I'll join you and relieve you of your burden. After our honeymoon, I will return with her to her father's house, and implore his blessing, with all the fatted calf offerings on his side.

WOOD. All right; but one thing, I use no more choloroform on that girl. The last time I thought that I had killed her, and it made me feel pretty shaky. I'm a pretty tough citizen, but I draw the line at murder; and I believe that another dose of that stuff would rob you of your bride.

GARDNER. Well, arrange it among yourselves; I must be off, or some of my search party may come this way. I will tell them that further search this way will be useless, and so will return and give you a free field. Good night, Daddy Carey, you and Woodruff settle your money affairs. Good night, mother.

CAREY. I'd better go with you to the ledge, Captain; the boys are on the lookout for service men, so be ready, and quick with the pass word. I'll see that you get out of here all right. (*goes to door.*)

WOOD. And I'll go with you. Damned if I feel comfortable in this place. (*Exit*, D. F., *first*, GARDNER; *then* CAREY, *then* WOOD.)

MOTHER C. (*watching them off.*) What's that he said about money? A package of money on the little lady--and I am to help take it from her. I get their cuffs, and kicks and hard words, for no one cares for an old useless creature like me. But when a woman's hand is needed, then they remember old Mother Carey. How that poor little lady looked into my old eyes, and spoke the first kind word I have heard for years. The first God's blessing since my poor daughter, just such another girl as she, was brought home to die. Her life had been a hard one, brought up as she was in an atmosphere of vice and crime, but her last words weae: "Mother, you couldn't help it - God bless you." Shall this pretty girl, the darling of another mother, be sacrificed to a fate worse than death, to the cruelty of an inhuman monster? No; not if I can help it, and I think I can. (*goes to door.* Little lady; little lady.

FLOR. I am here; what is it?

MOTHER C. Be quiet. I fear they will return any minute; I will do my best to save you. Seem to submit to all they say; no harm will come to you. I have a plan that may prove successful, though I risk my life in attempting it

FLOR. Oh, don't do that old lady, don't bring harm upon yourself. I am young and a merciful providence will protect me, but you must not risk the vengeance of these men.

MOTHER C. Rather than see another victim sacrificed as my poor daughter was, I'd face death itself.

FLOR. They mean to harm me, then?

MOTHER C. They would rob you first, and then submit you to a living tortuous death, but fear nothing little one; do as I say, and if we do not escape, Old Mother Carey will die with you.

FLOR. But, what is your plan?

MOTHER C. You listen at this door, hear what I shall say to these villians and act the part that I would have you play. Do not lose courage but smile, though your heart be breaking. Remember what you have at stake; liberty, honor, yes, even life itself. (*As she hears voices of men returning, she goes back to fireplace and begins to laugh heartily, throwing apron over her head.*)

Enter WOODRUFF *and* CAREY.

WOOD. What is the matter with the aged party?

CAREY. (*coming down to left.*) What's the matter, you old fool, you're making noise enough to alarm the whole neighborhood.

MOTHER C. Oh, it's the queerest thing I ever heard of.

CAREY. And what is that?

MOTHER C. The way that lady is going on, in the strong room.

WOOD. What ails her now? Is she tearing things to pieces?

MOTHER C. Tearing? Why, she's been singing and laughing and seems as merry as a cricket.

WOOD. Can it be that her brain has been turned.

CAREY. Have her out here and let's have a look at her. (MOTHER CAREY *goes toward the door.*)

WOOD. But stop; first to arrange how to get the packet.

CAREY. Don't be foolish. Throw her down and take it from her. You're too squeamish about these women; wait till you've handled 'em like I have—eh! Mother.

MOTHER C. Yes, indeed, daddy—yes indeed.

WOOD. Easier said than done. This is no ordinary girl. If ever there was a devil in a woman, it's in her.

MOTHER C. (*speaking loudly.*) If you'd take the advice of an old woman what knows her own sex, you'd have no trouble.

CAREY. Shut up you old fool, you're growing crazy.

WOOD. Let her speak. What is it Mammy?

MOTHER C. Sugar will catch more flies than vinegar. She's in a good humor now; keep her in it. Ask her to come out here by the fire, and if she must be a prisoner, tell her to be a comfortable one. As she's so fond of singing in there, mayhap she'd give us a song out here. Ill mix some hotwhisky, and in her glass I'll put a drop or two of the elegant mixture the doctor gave me to make me sleep. When once she's asleep what's easier than to take the money from her? Divide it among yourselves, wrap her up, put her in a carriage and before daylight you'll be at Redding's Crossing.

CAREY. Darn it. old woman, you've got some sense left. I did not give you the credit for it - but have her out at once. (FLORENCE *sings in her room.*)

WOOD Well, I've heard that women were strange critters, but this one beats me, I'm beginning to like the girl myself. Bring her out mammy.

MOTHER C. (*as she crosses.*) All right, don't frighten her, be civil and we'll have the money in no time at all. (*goes to door.*) Come dearie, don't you want to come by the fire?

FLOR. (*coming to door.*) Indeed I do, it's cold and lonesome in there—the least you can do is to give me a little fire.

CAREY. That's the way to talk. I say mother, give her a drop of something to warm her up. Come sit down here gal, don't be scared.

FLOR. Scared, why bless you man I never was scared in my life,. Anxiety for others has made me weaken for an instant, but it never took me long to recover.

WOOD. Well you're a plucky woman.

FLOR. You think so?

WOOD. I know so. I've positive proof.

FLOR. Oh, you're the party who is doing the kidnapping. Well, I don't bear malice, but I would like to know what you are going to do with me.

WOOD. I'm only acting as an agent, so I can't say.

CAREY. Never mind that, let's be sociable; and say, young woman, since you are so fond of singing to yourself, suppose you give us a song. I say mother, give us some good hot tipple.

WOOD. (*goes to window.*) I'll open this window, it's getting hot here.

MOTHER C. Come deary, sing for the gentlemen.

FLOR. Certainly. (*Music. Sings two verses of song, during song MOTHER CAREY pours hot water from tea kettle into glasses, and puts sleeping draught in glasses of CAREY and WOODRUFF.*)

CAREY. Good, splendid, but that's a little too solemn. (*dog barks outside.*) What's that, some one coming? (*Goes to window and says aside to MOTHER CAREY.*) Did you fix the glasses?

MOTHER C. Yes. (*aside.*) And I've fixed you.

CAREY. Give us something lively new, young lady, and here's to your good health.

WOOD. My compliments, Miss.

FLOR. This seems a bit strange to be convivial with one's keepers, but I must be with you, so here's to the health of us all. (*she drinks.*) Maybe this song would suit you better. (*She sings two verses—they watch her attentively—and then sink gradually into a deep sleep,* MOTHER C. *by the fireplace watches them. At the conclusion of song turns to old woman, who motions her to be quiet.*)

MOTHER C. (*whispering to her.*) Wait; here lie down in front of the fire, the noise of unbolting the doors might awaken them, you lie where they can see you if they awake, then I can give some excuse.

Music. FLORENCE *lies down in front of fire, covers her face with handkerchief. Old woman goes stealthily up to door, opens it a little, then goes down stage. Frank pushes door open, goes to his mistress, pulls handkerchief from her face, she starts up, sees him, he pulls her by the dress to door*

MOTHER C. Be careful; be quiet, they may awake.

FLOR. Why, this is my dear old Tony that Frank has led to me. God bless you, Mother Carey, and my faithful friends.

CURTAIN.

ACT IV.

SCENE I. *Parlor in* ESTABROOK'S *mansion. Centre door, backed by hall, hat-rack etc. Piano* R. I. E. *Centre table,* L. C. I. *Elegant furnishings, bric-a-brac, and set to be made elaborate as possible. Music on rise of curtain.*

Enter MR. ESTABROOK, *hastily.*

ESTA. Well, I think everything is ready now, if the surprise I have in store for my daughter shall be carried out as I have planned it. The events of the last forty-eight hours have nearly unnerved me, but the necessity for bearing up under our troubles gave me the courage to fight it to the end.

Enter DINAH, C. D.

DINAH. Ef yo' please, Massa Estabrook, Mistah Sho't is in de hall and wishes to speak to yo'.

ESTA. Show him in at once. (*Exit* DINAH.) I will soon know if our plan has succeeded. Short has been indeed a trusty and faithful friend; without him I should have been indeed helpless in my hour of suffering.

Enter SHORT, C. D.

ESTA. Ah! my good friend, I am delighted to see you back. But tell me what news?

SHORT   Great and glorious news, Mr. Estabrook. Fortune has smiled upon us in every way. I have a great' surprise in store for you.

ESTA. Indeed. (*Aside*,) I will not tell him my good news. (*Aloud*.) But what is it, Short? I am all impatient to hear it.

SHORT. Now, don't hurry me. If there is anything that a Northern man objects to, after he has been in the south more than a month, it is to be hurried. The Southerner is slow naturally, but the acquired habit of indolence can only be likened to the non-progressive but ever cheerful snail.

ESTA. But tell me the result of your mission.

SHORT. I will; but give me time. I must begin at the very beginning. You remember, after our return from the unsuccessful hunt for Miss Florence, that your insisted that your misfortune had fallen upon you because you had sold little Manda in spite of the earnest entreaties of your daughter. Ruling me out of the search, which you proposed putting in the hands of a professional, and not an amateur detective, as you called me, you asked me to try to recover the little child. I thereupon took the next packet for New Orleans, where we supposed the child would be found.

ESTA. Yes but you have not had the time to make that journey.

SHORT. As I said before, fortune was with us, for we had not been six hours on the river when the pilot saw the Muscatine, the boat that left Roscoe Landing night before last with your niggers on board, stuck hard and fast in a sand bar. It seems that two boats left Roscoe landing at the same time, and that there was a rivalry between them. A most exciting race commenced directly when they started down the river. It was an even contest, and the Muscatine had all she could do to hold her own. Her pilot had sworn she would land first at Bayou Marie, but the chances seemed against her. The pilot, who thought his reputation at stake, determined on a bold stroke; so he ventured into a channel that he thought was known only to himself, by which he could cut off a half a mile. He had not taken into account the change in the current, and the first thing he knew the boat was hard and fast on the bar.

ESTA. And she stuck there?

SHORT. Yes; the rival boat refused assistance, and sailed by at full speed, amid the triumphant cries of passengers and crew. The boat I was on was the next to pass, and when I saw the signal of distress and recognized the boat, I knew that my journey was near its end. I found the speculator who had the children in charge, and he was more than glad to sell Manda at half the figure she brought at the sale.

ESTA. Then Gardner's purchase of her—

SHORT. Was only to gratify his desire to thwart Miss Florence in the purchase; strange conduct for a lover, or one who professed to care for her.

ESTA. There is something inexplicable about that man. His plantation is small, and its products meagre, yet he lives in a style far beyond our wealthy planters. He must have some other source of income.

SHORT. I dislike to speak about a man behind his back, but there's no good in that man, and you'll some day find it out.

ESTA. I hope not, although I would not wish him for a son-in-law. He is our near neighbor, and his interest in Florence, and his anxiety to find her rather softened me toward him.

SHORT. I hope it may be as you say, but Miss Florence, what of her?

ESTA. Here is one who can answer that question better than I. (*Music*)

Enter FLORENCE

SHORT. (*astonished.*) Miss Florence here?

FLOR. Indeed yes, Mr. Short, you look at me as though I was something supernatural.

SHORT. Well, I confess that you seem to have returned from the grave.

FLOR. Do I look as sepulchral as that? Well then, my looks belie my feelings, for I never was quite as happy in my life.

SHORT. But where were you? What were you doing, who stole you, when— ?

FLOR. Talk of woman's curiosity, I could not answer all these questions at once; you shall know all in good time, but why were you not here to receive me? Mr Short you are ungallant.

SHORT. It was not my fault Miss Florence, I was executing a commission for your father.

ESTA. (*motioning to keep silent.*) Ahem!

SHORT. (*confused.*) That is I thought I would. Well, I just took a trip down the river, I wasn't feeling well and I thought a change of air—

FLOR. Mr. Short, I knew men were born to deceive, but deception sits badly upon your shoulders, and you, my dear old papa, have some secret for me.

ESTA. Secret my dear, not at all; very absurd, ha! ha!

SHORT. Yes indeed, very absurd, ha! ha!

FLOR. And I say you're both very absurd, ha, ha, to try to keep it from me. Now there's a good Mr. Short (*coaxingly*.) and there's a good papa, won't you tell me all about it.

ESTA. I never did see such a girl to wheedle an old man.

SHORT. Or a young man either, but I like it.

ESTA. I suppose we had better tell her.

SHORT. If she will say nothing about it at present.

FLOR. Oh, I'll promise.

ESTA. Then come with us, and we'll show you, but don't breathe a word about it.

FLOR. Not a word.

ESTA. Then come with me. (*they go well up to side door.*) I never did see such a girl, to coax and have her own way.

FLOR. And you like it.   (*Exit with* ESTABROOK.

SHORT. Oh, the way she said, "there's a good Mr. Short." By all that's lovely, I will marry that girl, if I have to steal her myself.

                                        (*Exit hastily*

Enter RASTUS, *dressed up.*

RASTUS. As dey say in de scripter, de prodigal son am return-ed, and deys fixed me up fer de fatted calf, but how's de calf gwine git fat 'less he git somfin' ter eat? Dere's done bin so much jol'fer-cation 'round dis'yer place dat dey fo'git dis nigger got 'sorbin' appe-tite. I'se so hungry dat my stumick 'spects my froat is cut; and ebery time I tell Dinah I'se hungry she say, go 'way, nigger, ain't yo' 'shamed so be hungry sich a time as dis'yer? I ain't had nuffin' ter eat but a crab apple since mawnin', and I ain't got no mo' struggle in me dan a mouse.

Enter DINAH, R. 2. E.

Look heah, Aunt, when yo' gwine give me my breakfus'?

DINAH. Dar yo' go 'gin. In dis time ob 'citement, when we's all tryin' to prepare fo' de missy's welcome, yo' do nuffin' but talk 'bout breakfus'

RASTUS. Breakfus'; dere's only one word w'at I know, dat souns, bettah dan breakfus', and dat's dinner.

DINAH. Well, we'll hab breakfus', dinner and supper altogeder after a w'ile. Yo' stir 'round and help us wid de preparations fo' de visitors, and if yo' is too lazy fo' dat, yo' go down to de stables and feed de mules.

RASTUS. Dar it goes 'gin. Feed de mules; 'deed I did feed de mules, and it made me cry w'en I seed 'em eatin' to t'ink dat a foah-legged jackass wus bettah treated dan a two-legged nigger. Wish I wus a jackass,

DINAH. Well, I done gib yo' warnin' dat ef massa heahs yo' groanin' 'round like dat, he'll skin yo' black hide. Now go down to de kitchin and help me and Jeff wid de supper.

RASTUS. Golly! dats a word I done fo'git all about. Breakfus' and dinner is all right in dere way, but gib me supper, good supper. I'll be wid yo' Aunt Dinah. (*Exit*, R. 1. E.

DINAH. Dat boy 'll neber come to no good. I neber did see sech o'nery nigger; allers eatin' and sleepin'; dere nevah was sech a lazy nigger in de worl'. Whar's dat ol' man ob mine? He's jess 'bout as bad. He's neber de same man sence dey took away little Manda; he 'pears to be grievin' mo' and mo' as de days pass by. Jeff! (*goes to door*,) Whar is yo' Jeff?

Enter JEFF.

JEFF. Heah I is. Dinah.

DINAH. W'at yo' gwine 'round wid sech a glum face fo' w'en dey's all happy kaze de little missy has come home?

JEFF. I kaint help it, Dinah. It makes me t'ink de mo' ob our little Manda. I know yo' feel as bad as I do, but you're tryin' to cheer me up. It seems as ef I'd gib my life to see dat little gal agin.

Enter FLORENCE, C. D.

FLOR. What was that you said, Uncle Jeff?

JEFF. Nuffin', missy. I wan't complainin', missy, 'deed I wan't.

FLOR. I know you was not complaining, but what would you say if I were to tell you that you would see your Manda again?

DINAH. See Manda! Oh, missy, say it agin.

JEFF. What would I say, missy? W'y I would bress de Lord, and t'ank him ebery day fo' his goodness, and I'd pray fo' yo' Missy Flo'ence; you'se alwus been de good angel to us poo' folks. But, tell us missy, is our little one comin' back?

FLOR. Indeed she is; she is here already, see– (*goes to* C. D., *brings down* MANDA, *who rushes to* DINAH *and* JEFF.)

JEFF. God bress de lamb and God brese yo', Missy Flo'ence; de Lord has done answer my pra'rs, an' brought dis little one back safe home to us.

FLOR. But now you must haste and and prepare for our visitors. Papa has invited them to celebrate my safe return, and we want none but happy faces around us. Dinah, take Manda down to the kitchen, and Uncle Jeff, you must have your banjo ready, for we want you to amuse us.

JEFF. 'Deed I will, missy; dere's not a happier man in all dis worl' dan I am, and de bes' de ol' banjo can do will be done dis night. Come, Manda. De Lord bress de little missy. (*Exit* R. 2. E.

DINAH. De ol' man is so powerful glad dat he doan gib me a chance to t'ank yo', Missy Flo'ence. May yo' life be as happy as yo' hab made us poo' colla'd folks. (*kissing the hand of* FLORENCE.)

(*Exit,* R. 2. F.

FLOR. How happy they are to get back their child. I can now realize the anguish of my own parents while my fate was still in doubt. It all seems like a terrible dream; the struggle on the road, and the imprisonment in that horrible place. I shall never forget the agony of that night. That poor old woman; she was indeed my friend. She said she would leave the den that night, and come to me; I will see that her life is made as comfortable as possible in return for the good service she rendered me.

Enter SHORT, *speaking up stage.*

SHORT. (*aside.*) Ah, there she is, and alone. This is my only chance, but I feel as bashful as a school-boy. (*aloud.*) Ah, Miss Florence, did you execute your part of our plan?

FLOR. Yes, Mr. Short, and the parents are overjoyed. I suppose they are weeping afresh over their baby, and when I saw the happiness of those poor people in the recovery of their child, I realized what my father and mother must have endured in my sbsence.

SHORT. You will never know the depth of our misery, Miss Florence. You will not think me presumptious, I hope, when I say *our* misery, for every hour you was gone seemed to me a day, and when I saw your sweet face again, it was as if the sun had burst from behind the clouds and illumined the earth again.

FLOR. Why, Mr. Short, you are quite poetical, but I must grant you some licence. My hope was in you while I was a prisoner, but my detective failed me.

SHORT. I confess it; but the end has not yet come. Our principal movement you happily anticipated by galloping home with your faithful horse and dog, but now I propose to find the miscreants who committed the dastardly outrage and bring them to justice.

FLOR. Have you a clue?

SHORT. Only a slight one, yet it may become a hint or suggestion for a line of circumstantial evidence.

FLOR And it is--?

SHORT. Only a handkerchief, but of peculiar pattern and nearly covered with blood. I found it quite a distance on this side of Johnston's Glen, and kept it for future use. It may lead to the capture and punishment of the criminals.

FLOR. I hope you will succeed, but I am too happy to think or talk of vengeance now.

SHORT. And I am so happy to have you back that I hardly

know whether I am standing on my head or heels.

FLOR. My father has told me how active you were in the search for me, and what warm friends you and he have grown to be in the past two weeks. I am deeply grateful, Mr. Short.

SHORT. But I did nothing, Miss Florence. If I only could have followed the trail and rescued you from the moonshiner's den, I would have been the happiest mortal on the earth.

FLOR. Happy to have gratified your ambition to shine as a detective, I suppose?

SHORT. No, happy to have been of service to you, and to have contributed to your happiness by any means in my power.

FLOR. Thank you, Mr. Short. I appreciate your feeling and have always held you in the highest esteem. Believe me, I fully share my father's opinion of you. You are quite a hero in his eyes.

SHORT. I would that I appeared so in yours.

FLOR. Why, Mr. Short, I believe you are growing serious.

SHORT. More serious than I have ever been in my life before. I am—well, to make a clean breast of it—I'm in love.

FLOR. In love? Why, Mr. Short, I thought you were only devoted to your different professions.

SHORT. Now, Miss Florence, don't laugh at me. I know it is presumptious in me to press my suit on short acquaintance. I have broached the subject to your father, he has not discouraged me. I dare to ask you if you will give me hope.

FLOR. You remember the old saying, while there's life there's hope.

SHORT. Then I may ?

FLOR. You may.

SHORT. (*embracing her.*) Oh, Florence, you have made me the happiest man in the word.

Enter RASTUS, C. D.

RASTUS. Ahem! Achos! Oh, golly! I didn't see nuffin'—I'se foolish, I is.

FLOR. (*startled and flushed.*) Rastus, What are you doing here?

RASTUS. I jes' doin' nuffin'.

SHORT. You should have bells on your feet, Rastus, so that people can hear you coming.

RASTUS. Golly, he takes me fer a goat. I wus jes' gwine to tell yo' dat massa say dat de folks is a comin'.

SHORT. You are a little late with your information, for here they are.

FLOR. Who, Rastus?

RASTUS. Mistah Gardner and 'nudder strange gemman.

SHORT. Well, we don't want to see them just yet, so Miss Florence, let us slip into the next room. There's something about that man that I don't like.

FLOR. And I hate him.   (*Exit with* SHORT, R. 2. E.

RASTUS. (*imitating both.*) 'N I jus consoquechally dispise him.

Enter GARDNER *and* WOODRUFF, *clean shaven and nicely dressed.*

GARDNER. I say, Rastus, help me with my coat and then announce us to your master. (*servant hangs coat on rack back of* C. D.

RASTUS. Who'll I say is wid yo' Mistah Gardner?

GARDNER. Say a friend and be quick about it. Do you hear?

RASTUS. Yes sah, I heah; I'se un'standin' ef I is foolish. (*Exit.*

GARDNER. Well, you made a pretty mess of that matter. Three of you to one woman, and yet she outwitted you, and robbed me of my revenge.

WOOD. But, what is your purpose in coming here? I cannot understand.

GARDNER. We have lost the money, but I have not finished with her yet. It would look suspicious to remain away on an occasion of this kind, so I have come to extend my congratulations, and to introduce you as a friend who has just arrived from the North. You could nowhere be safer than here, and we must find some way to carry out my plans; for that girl I must and will have.

WOOD. Take my advice and give it up. You have lost the confidence of the gang by last night's work. Daddy Carey and his chickens, as he calls them, have taken to the mountain, fearing arrest.

GARENER So much the better. If a search is instituted they will find the house empty. But what became of the old lady?

WOOD. When we had awakened from our stupor she had disappeared. It was all her fault, for she drugged our glasses instead of the girl's. She knew that the job was worth her life, so she's gotten out of the way.

GARDNER. No more of this. Here comes Mr. Estabrook.

Enter ESTABROOK.

ESTA. I am pleased to see you, Mr. Gardner. You are a welcome guest at our little celebration.

GARDNER. Allow me to introduce Mr. Woodruff, of Louisville, Ky. He is my guest, and I took the liberty of bringing him with me.

ESTA. Any friend of Mr. Gardner's is heartily welcome. When did you arrive, Mr. Woodruff?

WOOD. Last night.

GARDNER. Yes, and I have just been explaining to him the significance of this little gathering. Believe me, Mr. Estabrook, I never heard of such an occurrence. To think that such an outrage should be perpetrated in our vicinity is almost incredible.

ESTA. But true nevertheless. And here comes the heroine of the adventure.

Enter FLORENCE R. 2. E., *with* SHORT.

GARDNER. Miss Florence, I come to congratulate you on your plucky escape from your abductors and safe return to your home.

FLOR. (*coldly.*) Thank you, sir. (*crosses stage.*)

SHORT. (*aside.*) Cool and bracing.

ESTA. (*bringing* WOODRUFF *forward.*) Florence, this is Mr. Woodruff of Louisville, a friend of Mr. Gardner.

FLOR. I am pleased to know you, sir.

WOOD. I am charmed to meet so courageous a lady as the heroine of the story Mr. Gardner has been telling me.

FLOR. Have we ever met before?

WOOD. I think not; why do you ask?

FLOR. Oh, nothing; probably a mere fancy. Your voice seems strangely familiar.

GARDNER. (*aside.*) Can she suspect? No, impossible!

ESTA. Florence dear, I have promised your friends that they shall hear of your adventure from your own lips.

FLOR. With pleasure; but we have first a little musicale, after which I shall be pleased to tell my wonderful adventures.

Enter MRS. ESTABROOK, *visitors, &c. Specialties by* JEFF, SHORT *and* RASTUS.

GARDNER. And now, Miss Florence, we are anxious to hear all about your strange adventure.

ESTA. Yes, Florence, even your mother and I have not heard all the particulars.

SHORT. Please give us the full details, Miss Florence. You know I must redeem my failure to find you, by bringing your abductors to justice. I have already been sworn in as a deputy and am empowered to make arrests.

GARDNER. Oh, then you are to be the detective in this case Mr. Short. I hope you are well supplied with clues?

FLOR. Mr. Short has not much in the way of evidence, but I think he is on the right track. Before I begin, however, I must have the real hero to substantiate my story. Rastus, will you bring Frank to me?

RASTUS. Yes, Missy, I'll hab 'im heah bery soon. (*Exit* R. 2 E.

WOOD. (*aside to* GARDNER.) Do you think they suspect?

GARENER Nonsense. Our very presence here would save us from suspicion.

ESTA. To think that the dog should have been the means of bringing back my daughter to me.

FLOR. You see, Mr. Gardner, it is well to have the friendship of a dog; even the one you thought deserving of nothing but blows, a few days ago.

GARDNER. I trust you do not bear malice on that score. I see my error, and will cheerfully beg pardon of the noble animal. (*aside.*) Curse the dog, I would like to poison him!

Enter Frank, followed by RASTUS.

RASTUS. Dar he is, missy, an' mighty proud to see yo', sho 'nuff.

FLOR. (*caressing him.*) Dear old faithful friend, you shall come and kiss your mistress. (*patting him.*) Now be a good dog. Come, Mr. Gardner, and make your peace with him.

GARDNER. (*approaching. Frank growls. Taking handkerchief from his pocket and rubbing his hand.*) He evidently is not fond of me, but I trust he will learn to like me.

SHORT. Pardon my Yankee curiosity, Mr. Gardner; I have been admiring that little handkerchief. May I see it?

GARDNER. Certainly. It is of a peculiar pattern. A dozen of them were sent me by a friend in Paris—but come, Miss Florence, you are forgetting the story.

FLOR. (*sitting* R. C.—*dog lying at her feet.*) Well, to begin; as you have doubtless heard, my father had a package of money and securities that he was desirous of sending to New Orleans. The boat left Roscoe Landing at nine o'clock of the evening of the sale, and he delayed sending it until it was almost too late. I, anxious to show him that I was repentant for opposing his will, regarding the child, Manda

GARDNER. Who is now in New Orleans, happy and forgetful of her parents and home.

FLOR. You are mistaken. Manda is here, happy and rejoicing with her parents.

GARDNER. (*aside.*) Thwarted even in that.

FLOR. The night was dark and I was timid at first, but with my noble Tony and faithful Frank as companions, I felt that I had little to fear. Tony seemed to know that we had been entrusted with an important mission, for never did he cover the ground so quickly; we flew like the wind. Near the rocky pass before reaching Johnston's

Glen he was obliged to slacken his pace and pick his way more carefully, when suddenly a figure arose from the darkness, seized the bridle, and demanded that I should stop. Robbery was the object, for the man asked the surrender of the package. I would rather have given my life than to have given it up. After I had been torn from my horse I offered my jewels for my release, but an accomplice of the villain took my medallion and put it in his pocket. (*At these words Frank goes up stage to coat.*) Why, Frank are you deserting me? Come here, old fellow.

GARDNER. (*aside.*) What can the dog be doing?

FLOR. Ah, that is one of his old tricks. He heard me speak of pockets, and you know what a skillful pick-pocket he is. See, he is taking something from the pocket. Bring it here old fellow. (*takes paper.*) Why, it is a piece of paper with something inside. May I open it?

GARDNER. Certainly—it's only an old envelope.

FLOR. Why it's father, Mr. Short everybody--see here is the medallion that was stolen from me at Johnston's Glen—and there stands the robber!

ALL. Gardner!!

GARDNER. What is the meaning of all this—you surely would not accuse me of such a crime?

SHORT. That's just what we do, Mr. Gardner. The dog has proven the first point. I will prove the second.

GARDNER. You!

SHORT. Yes, me. This handkerchief that you just gave me is a mate to this one, (*pulling out handkerchief.*) stained with blood, and found near the old hut where you tied the dog.

GARDNER. Ridiculous.

SHORT. You think so? Then where did you get that scar on your hand?

GARDNER. That—why, that's a scratch from the brush.

SHORT. You lie! It is the mark of a bite from this dog.

GARDNER. Absurd. You are making a most unjust and terrible accusation. You say the object of the abduction was robbery; you must confess I knew nothing of the money, or this woman's journey to Roscoe. I wasn't near this place on that night.

RASTUS. Yes yo' wus, Mistah Gardner, fer I seed yo' w'en I went fer Missy's hoss dat night. I seed yo' jump frum de window an' git on yo'r hoss at de stables.

SHORT, The evidence is strong enough to warrant an arrest. Mr. Gardner, you are my prisoner. Rastus, get a couple of men to take charge of this man until we can take him to Roscoe. (*Enter slaves-- men hold* GARDNER.)

WOOD. (*Aside.*) It's time for me to be off. (*Aloud.*) Mr. Estabrook I regret this. I had no idea of my friend's complicity in this affair; my presence here must be unwelcome, so I will go.

FLOR. Not yet.

WOOD. And why, Miss Estabrook.

FLOR. I told you your voice was familiar, and now I recall the time we met. You are the man who carried me to Carey's den.

WOOD. I? You mistake me. I only arrived last night, and who can verify your suspicion?.

Enter MOTHER CAREY, C. D.

MOTHER C. I can. I know you in spite of your shaven face and your good clothes. You are Frank Woodruff, and that is the Captain of the band of moonshiners whose headquarters were at Carey's den.

FLOR. Mother Carey! You here?

MOTHER C. Yes, dear child. I knew it was certain death to remain in that den any longer, so I followed you on foot. I hid in the woods by day and walked at night, until I found your house, know-you would protect me.

FLOR. Indeed I will, and this shall be your home the rest of your days. This dear old woman, father, saved me from a living death.

ESTA. You are indeed welcome, my good woman.

SHORT. Rastus, a couple attendants for this gentleman.

RASTUS. Heah dey is, Massa Sho't—w'at will we do wid him an' todder feller?

SHORT. Take them to the stable and bind them; we will soon have them safely lodged in Roscoe jail.

RASTUS. Come 'long, Mistah Gardner and todder feller, we'll put yo's in a place whar yo's won't break yo's necks by fallin' out ob de winders.   (*Exit* WOODRUFF, C. D., *with guard.*

GARDNER. The game is up, but I have ruined you, you old aristocrat. Your name is dishonored. I have at least that revenge.

(*Exit, led off by guard.*

RASTUS. I neber did like dat man, but I'se foolish.   *Exit.*

ESTA. He is right, I am dishonored; but I can still make good my indebtedness.

SHORT. Excuse me, Mr. Estabrook, here is a letter I brought from Roscoe. (*hands letter.*) Pardon my forgetting it in the excitement, until now.

ESTA. (*looking over letter.*) Good news again. Stocks have taken another turn, and my obligations were met by the brokers out of the proceeds. Mr. Short, you have proved yourself a friend, in all this period of gloom and uncertainty. How can I reward you?

SHORT. With this young lady's hand. She has already given me hope.

FLOR. And with papa's consent, here it is, with my heart in it

ESTA. Take her, Short. She will prove the best of wives, as I know you will make her an excellent husband.

FLOR. But in our happiness we must not forget those who have so largely contributed to it—Mother Carey, dear old Toney and Frank—OUR FAITHFUL FRIENDS.

CURTAIN.

www.ingramcontent.com/pod-product-compliance
Lightning Source LLC
Chambersburg PA
CBHW031320280626
47169CB00019B/2511